SEASONS REMEMBERED

A TIME TO SPEAK

Linda Shands

D0123806

IVP

InterVarsity Press
Downers Grove, Illinois

InterVarsity Press® is the book-publishing division of InterVarsity Christian Fellowship®, a
student movement active on campus at hundreds of universities, colleges and schools of nursing in
the United States of America, and a member movement of the International Fellowship of
Evangelical Students. For information about local and regional activities, write Public Relations
Dept., InterVarsity Christian Fellowship, 6400 Schroeder Rd., P.O. Box 7895, Madison, WI
53707-7895.

Cover illustration: David Darrow
ISBN 0-8308-1934-7

Printed in the United States of America

Library of Congress Cataloging-in-Publication Data

Shands, Linda, 1944-
    A time to speak/Linda Shands.
       p.   cm.—(Seasons remembered)
     ISBN 0-8308-1934-7 (pbk.: alk. paper)
    I. Title. II. Series: Shands, Linda, 1944-   Seasons remembered.
  PS3569.H329T575   1996
  813'54—dc20   95-48941
                                        CIP

17	16	15	14	13	12	11	10	9	8	7	6	5	4	3	2	1
10	09	08	07	06	05	04	03	02	01	00	99	98	97	96		

To Mom and Dad Shands
in loving memory

Prologue

Memorial Day, 1970

Dear Dotty,

We took Jesse to the cemetery with us today. Not the most exciting outing for a seven-year-old, but he had helped us pick the flowers from the garden and insisted on coming along. "We learned about Memorial Day in school," he said, "and it's about time I learned to respect the dead." He meant "pay his respects," of course, and I had to pinch myself to keep from laughing.

Rose Hills is a beautiful place. Jesse thought it looked like a park, and I suppose it does with the rolling, green hills and all those trees. The garden at the entrance was in full bloom, and he wondered why we couldn't have picked our flowers there.

We drove clear up to Mountain of Prayer Avenue, where Mama and Papa are buried. I know it doesn't matter, but I always felt the first to go should be the first we visit. Besides, there's such a clear view from there.

We didn't take Jesse to the most recent grave. My grief is still too new, and I didn't want to break down in front of him.

We did scatter flowers, though—white daisy petals, for the ones buried in other places. I laid a red carnation on a soldier's grave and prayed for you and Sam.

As King Solomon said, "To everything there is a season, and a time to every purpose under the heaven." Well, we've certainly seen most of it, haven't we, girl? Seeing those graves today brought back so many memories. Every decade's marked by something different. The Depression in the thirties. Remember when I came to live with Aunt Rose and Uncle Edward? You were my first and best friend—and still are today, even if you live so far away. Then the forties: Pearl Harbor, and that awful war. I married Jake and you married Sam. The Four Musketeers. Who could know we'd someday live three thousand miles apart?

It was in the fifties we finally found my brother Chuck and sister Grace, after searching for so long. And things turned out to be so different than I'd thought they would. But that's the way life is, isn't it? The good Lord must think we'd die of boredom if he didn't stir things up a bit. For me it was one mixed-up extended family. For you it was six kids! I can keep the whole bunch straight, but I don't even try to sort them out for someone else anymore.

I think it's the decade just past, though, that held the most changes. Our parents would have never thought of satellites and guided missiles, or rockets to the moon. And all the violence! I'm glad Mama wasn't around to see the riots, a president killed right on TV. And Vietnam, of course. The scars from that will never go away.

I read the rest of Solomon's words today. "A time to be born, a time to die . . . a time to kill, a time to heal . . . a time to love, a time to hate . . . a time of war, a time of peace." The last ten years have certainly been all of that. But, as you know now, the years 1961 through 1963 were a season all their own for me, and my grandson has a way of keeping those memories alive.

* * *

Jesse studied the plain granite headstones. "Charles Ray Summers, 1898-1936, and Lynetta May Summers, 1903-1948. My great-grandpa and grandma, right?" He looked so proud of himself for figuring it out.

"That's right," I said, and handed him one of the metal containers we had just filled with water. "Would you like to put the flowers in?"

He nodded and reached for one of the bouquets. "I think Great-grandma should have this one. It's the prettiest, and she liked pretty things."

"Why yes, she did," I said. "How did you guess?"

He looked solemn. "I didn't guess. Mama told me. She said Great-grandma was sick a lot and didn't always know where she was. She lived in a sana—sanatorium where she was surrounded by nice thoughts and pretty things."

I smiled. Leave it to Libby. She had such a knack for phrasing things and always seemed to know what to say to a child.

I handed him the second bouquet—mostly carnations and greenery. He unwrapped the newspaper and set the flowers in the container at the head of Papa's grave. "Was Great-grandpa really framed for murder?" he asked out of the blue. His eyes, round and black as olives, sparked with excitement and a hint of pride.

Oh grief, I thought, *what has Libby told him?* Libby was all of fourteen before we told her how my papa died. It's not easy to explain to a child that her grandfather had been involved in an embezzlement scheme and sent to prison.

"Mama said some gangsters told the cops Great-grandpa killed a guy, and that he died in prison even though it wasn't true. Is that what happened, Gram?"

"Yes," I said, bending to brush a smear of mud from my grandson's knee. "We'd best go on now. We've got two more bouquets to deliver."

I didn't want to talk about Roy Cummings, his involvement with my mother, or the baby buried back in Pike, Nevada, out on Harris Hill. Roy was the one who had schemed to get my papa killed. Then he was killed himself, by the very thugs he thought were his friends. I shuddered and felt a small hand slip into mine. "I'm sorry, Gram. Does it make you sad?"

"Sometimes." I forced a smile. "But that's all right. Everybody gets sad now and then."

We drove down to Peaceful Valley Lane. The breeze picked up just as we came to Jake's father's plot and scattered seed pods from the eucalyptus trees across the headstone.

Jesse bent down and swept them away. "How come these are iron? You can't read them as good."

"They're brass, sweetie. They're newer than the others."

I expected him to wrinkle his nose and holler "I'm not a sweetie!" like he usually did, but he was concentrating so hard on the marker, he must not have heard.

"Delbert Freeman, 1896-1961. That means Great-grandpa Freeman was sixty-five when he died."

I took a deep breath. "That's right," I said. "He went to be with Jesus just a year and a half before you were born."

Jesse's forehead wrinkled. "Mama says that's why Jesus sent me—to take Great-grandpa Freeman's place. She says I'm a gift from God. Is that true, Gram?"

I could tell he wasn't sure he wanted it to be. I closed my eyes a moment, then bent down and took hold of his arms. "Look at me, Jesse," I said softly. He obeyed. "I don't know if God sent you to take Grandpa Freeman's place, but your mama is right: you are a gift from God. And don't ever let anyone tell you different."

His eyes lit up and he hugged me hard. "Okay, Gram, I promise." He pushed away and grinned. "Cross my heart and hope to die, stick a needle in my eye." His giggle swelled to full-blown laughter, and the wind blew it, echoing, across the rolling hills.

Chapter One

If Pa Freeman hadn't passed away, Libby would probably have stayed with my aunt Rose and maybe, just maybe, the rest of it wouldn't have happened. But Jake's father did die. On January 1, 1961.

Libby had talked me into taking her to the Rose Parade that day. It was held in Pasadena, just a few miles from our home in San Gabriel, California.

Jake and I usually stayed home and watched it on TV. "Why should we fight all those people and sit on a curb with our feet in the gutter when we can see it just as well from here?" was how he put it. And I had to agree. Besides, Dotty and I always took the girls to Victory Park afterward to see the floats, while the guys watched football on television.

But Libby had been so disappointed when her friend Carol's family canceled their plans for the parade and went to their grandmother's for New Year's instead. "Please, Mom?" she had wheedled. "I didn't get to go last year either. It's not like it costs anything."

Only a few hours' sleep. But I gave in. Goodness knows, at sixteen she seldom wanted my company anymore; I should probably have felt honored by her request.

Chapter One

In the end I was glad we went, even though the clouds hung low and threatened rain. By the time we got home, we were laughing and cutting up like school chums. We were still laughing as we raced from the garage to the back porch, dodging raindrops the size of dimes.

Jake was sitting at the kitchen table and glaring at his coffee cup, his shaved-smooth face as gloomy as the darkening sky.

Libby grabbed a tea towel to pat her hair. The auburn locks she had taken such pains to tease and spray that morning were damp and sticky. She took one look at her father and headed for the bathroom. "I'm going to wash my hair," she called, and shut the door.

I sighed and draped my coat over a kitchen chair. Lately Jake bounced from sweetness and light to gloom and doom at a snap of the fingers. I couldn't imagine what had upset him now. He'd been perfectly happy when we'd left him, hovering over the coffeepot and scanning the morning *Examiner.*

I stepped up behind him and kissed the top of his head. His hair had thinned a little, and his sideburns were peppered with gray. Still, he looked pretty good for a man of forty-one. "What's the matter, darling? Did we get you up too early?"

His scowl deepened. "Dave's back home. Ma called this morning to ask if I could help him find a job."

Jake's youngest brother had turned twenty-four in December, but he still hadn't settled down. He shouted to the heavens about freedom and independence, but he couldn't keep a job. He was in and out of his parents' house like a mongrel stray.

"Why do they let him come and go like that?" Jake was incensed. "If it were my house, he'd be on the street so fast his head would swim!"

I sighed and rubbed the muscle in his shoulder. It was pouring outside now, and I knew his old injuries caused him no end of pain in the cold and damp. "You're not a mother," I said gently. "What if it were Libby? Would you kick her out when she couldn't support herself?"

Jake shrugged my hand away. "For Pete's sake, Celia, that's different. Libby's a girl. Anyway, she's in school where she belongs. Not out chasing God-knows-where on some motorcycle and hanging out with a gang of loser thugs."

He drained his coffee cup and held it out for a refill. I emptied the pot into his cup and watched him stir in two teaspoonfuls of sugar. "You know, sugar isn't good for you."

He ignored my chiding and went on with his tirade. "What really gets me is that Pa puts up with it, lets the little twerp come and go at will. And Ma . . ." He shook his head and let the sentence go unfinished.

All I could do was give his shoulder one last squeeze. "Would you like more coffee? I can make another pot."

He looked blank, then forced a smile and handed me the empty cup. "No thanks, babe." He looked at his watch. "I don't have time. I told the Wilkersons I'd have their radiator by tomorrow morning." He must have seen the look on my face, because he stood up and tweaked my chin. "Don't fuss. I've been home two weekends in a row. This was an emergency. Anyway, we gotta build up that vacation fund!"

Vacation fund! I'd been hearing about this mysterious bank account for years. And hearing the promises too: "Fun and sun, babe—two whole weeks in paradise. It'll be worth it, wait and see." But I'd been waiting, and the great vacation had yet to materialize. I couldn't help but wonder if it ever would. Jake meant well, but his dreams were usually much bigger than his means.

I watched him push his arms into his jacket and trudge, head down, into the blowing rain. He'd be soaked by the time he reached the garage.

Sighing, I hung my coat up in the hall closet and turned my attention to my own appearance. I had to stand on tiptoe to see in the mirror Jake had hung in the entryway.

My hair was honey-blond, a bit darker than it had been when I was young, and I'd had it cut just below the ears. It needed a wash and set, but it wasn't as scraggly as Libby's. My nose and forehead were still dusted with freckles; I'd given up trying to get rid of them years ago. My brows and lashes were a good two shades lighter than my hair. Without the makeup I'd been too lazy to put on at four o'clock that morning, my features almost disappeared. "You better stay on good terms with the Avon Lady," Dotty had teased, "because without mascara and eyebrow pencil, you're doomed."

I went back to the kitchen to tackle the breakfast dishes, vowing to fix my face as soon as Libby was through in the bathroom.

My thoughts drifted back to the Freemans. Jake was right. Dave's behavior upset his mother terribly, and I knew it was a serious strain on his father as well. Anne Marie, Jake's oldest sister, was a nurse, and she'd confided that Pa had been suffering from chest pains lately. "He says it's indigestion," she told me on the phone last week, "and I suppose it could be. But last time I was down I convinced him to let me check his blood pressure, and it was sky high. He promised to go to the doctor, but you know Pa; he probably just said it to get me out of his hair."

The ringing telephone interrupted my thoughts.

"I'll get it!" Libby yelled, and I smiled when the phone was silenced after the second ring. She must have been expecting a call from Ron, the young sailor Carol had introduced her to. They'd been double-dating with Carol and her boyfriend whenever the boys were in town. Libby assured us it was nothing serious. "Honestly, Mom," she said once, after they had all been here for Sunday dinner, "I think you like him more than I do!" He was a nice young man. If parents could still pick their daughter's husband . . . I smiled at the thought but vowed not to share it with Libby. She wouldn't be amused.

"Mom?"

Libby stood in the doorway between the dining room and kitchen, her face white as the tissue she was wadding up between shaking hands.

"Libby, what's wrong?"

"Mom," she said again, "you better talk to Grandma Freeman. She says Grandpa fell off the roof. I think he's . . ." She covered her face with both hands, and I thought my heart would explode. I forced myself to hurry past my sobbing daughter and pick up the telephone.

Chapter
Two

The doctor said Pa Freeman died of a heart attack. He'd gone up on the roof, against Ma's protests, to fix the antenna. No one knew if he slipped on the wet shingles or if his heart gave out first.

We were gathered in the kitchen at the Freemans' house on York Street. Pa had passed away on Saturday, and by Monday noon the whole family had arrived. Jake was the oldest of eight children. His brother Tim had been killed in the war, but that left seven siblings, and two of the girls were married. It added up to quite a houseful.

Jake had insisted Libby go to school like usual. She fumed, but I backed him up. "There's nothing you can do today anyway," I said. "It's your first day back, and you'll have to miss tomorrow for the funeral."

Jake had made all the arrangements. We were relieved to discover there was insurance to cover the burial and enough left over to pay most of the bills. No one had brought the subject up, but we all knew something would have to be done: Ma couldn't manage alone for very long.

Poor Ma had seen it happen. She'd been there the whole time, holding the ladder steady and watching the television through the window to tell him when the screen was clear. "He had it fixed." She rubbed her eyes on the sleeve of her housedress and clutched her teacup in both hands. "I told him to watch his step coming down. He weren't no spring chicken anymore. Had no business monkeying around on that roof. I told him that too." She went quiet for a while.

Jake got up and paced the kitchen, then headed out the back door. He had to shove it open with his boot.

"Blamed thing's been stickin' for years," John piped up, following his brother out the door.

I sighed. For some illogical reason, Jake blamed his brother Dave—and himself—for their father's death.

"Just where was Dave when Pa went up on the roof?" he had said earlier. "For that matter, where was I? We both knew he was ill. Anne Marie as much as told us so. Dave knew the antenna was acting up the night before. He should have called me or fixed it himself."

I had tried to soothe him. "You know your father. He would never have let someone else take over his responsibilities." Nothing I said had seemed to make a difference.

Ma Freeman suddenly smiled and shook her head. "That man's a wonder," she said. "He was breathin' some when I got to him, and you know what he said?"

She was looking right at me, like there was no one else in the room. I put my hand on top of hers and went along with her memory. "What did he say?"

" 'Remember well, Ella, remember well.' 'What do you want me to remember?' I asked him. 'No!' he says and jerks his hand away like I'd stomped on his arm. 'Water,' he said then, and closed his eyes." She rubbed a work-calloused knuckle under her nose, and I handed her a tissue from the box on the table. "Here it is pouring rain all over both of us, and he asks for water. I couldn't get him to say no more."

Chapter Two

She laid her head down on the kitchen table. Anne Marie got up, wrapped her fingers around her mother's wrist and watched the second hand on the yellow plastic wall clock. After a while Anne Marie let go and smoothed her mother's hair. "Please don't fret about it. He hit his head, remember? He was bound to be confused. Let's get you up to bed now." She motioned to Brian, who came around and took his mother's arm.

John came in from the yard just then. "Jake wants you," he said, nodding in my direction.

I excused myself and hurried out the door.

* * *

I found Jake out by the boxwood hedge, standing still as stone and staring at the house next door. My house, once. So long ago, yet it seemed like yesterday. Jake would meet me at this very spot and we would talk the afternoon away—or push on through the gap in the hedge and lounge against the apple tree, munching his mother's homemade cookies and pointing out cloud pictures in the sky.

The house looked different now. Smaller somehow, even though one of the owners had added on. The yard was cluttered with soggy leaves and neglected children's toys. A rusty hoe leaned like a tired old man against the apple tree. I wondered if our initials were still there. Jake had carved them with his new pocketknife and had to take a scolding from Mama. "You put that knife away before you ruin that tree. Don't you know it's a living thing?" She pointed to the sap running from the wound. "See there, you've made it bleed." Jake nodded and tried to look repentant. But as soon as Mama went back into the house, he took the knife out and finished off the F for Freeman. $C S + J F$ in a double-outlined heart.

The break in the hedge had grown together over the last twenty-five years, separating the two houses as sure as any fence.

Jake didn't even turn his head, but he knew I was there. "What has Ma got to wear?"

"What?"

He looked annoyed. "To the funeral."

I hadn't given it a thought. And I'm sure no one else had thought to ask her what she had to wear tomorrow.

"I'd bet my boots she doesn't have anything decent." Jake reached into his pocket and handed me a wad of bills. "Here. John and I chipped in. We'll get more from the others later. Is that enough for a nice black dress?"

I counted out ten dollars in ones. "It should be, but where on earth will I find something now? It's almost eight o'clock."

"Then go in the morning." He turned to me, and even in the moonlight I could see his eyes were puffy-red. He looked tired and defeated. I wrapped my arms around his waist and pulled him close. For one quiet moment he rested his chin on my head. Then he pulled away. "Who all's staying the night?"

"Anne Marie, of course, and Sara June and Steven. Amy too, I think. The boys are going home."

Jake nodded. "Let's go home too, Cissy. Libby shouldn't be alone."

I wanted to say, "She's sixteen, she'll be just fine." Jake still thought of Libby as a little girl, and that had to change. But now was not the time to bring it up.

I thought it best not to mention Dave, either. He and Jake had had some words this morning, and before anyone could blink an eye, Dave had roared off on his motorcycle, leaving tire marks on the driveway. He hadn't been back. I could only hope he'd show up for the funeral bathed and sober.

Chapter Three

The Freemans' pastor pulled Jake aside before the funeral. When Jake came back to our seats in the family section at the Westside Presbyterian Church, his face held an odd expression. I asked him with my eyes, but he shook his head and pointed to the podium. The pastor had come to stand behind it, and a woman I didn't recognize began to sing "Beyond the Sunset."

I couldn't help but think how out of place her dark-blue tailored suit would have looked in the Freemans' living room. Pa Freeman's burial clothes were his Sunday best, but they were still threadbare; the mortician had had to patch a hole in one of the sleeves.

Libby's sobs broke my train of thought. Jake and I both put our arms around her, and the three of us huddled like nestlings taking shelter from a storm while the pastor reminded us that Delbert Jackson Freeman was now free from the struggles of this life and safe with Jesus in his heavenly home.

Dave sat on the end of the row, next to Brian, in a clean shirt and tie, his shaggy hair slicked back from his forehead with a generous helping of his father's VO5.

After the service and the burial, friends from church brought over pies and cakes and casseroles enough to feed the entire congregation. Ma insisted on organizing it all. She moved from kitchen to living room and back again, making sure everybody had their fill.

Dave's twin sister, Amy, cornered Jake and me in the dining room. "Shouldn't Ma be lying down or something? We should be waiting on her."

I started to say, "Leave her be, she needs to stay busy," when Anne Marie moved up beside us. She had deep blue circles below her eyes, like she'd been in the ring with Floyd Patterson and lost. "Jake, I'm sorry to butt in, but Dave grabbed a six-pack and went out back over an hour ago. He needs some food in his stomach, but he won't listen to me."

Jake's shoulders sagged, then straightened as he drew a long deep breath. To steady nerves, or temper? Probably both. I thought for a minute he would tell his sister just to leave Dave alone, but instead he squeezed her hand and headed for the door.

"Are you sure that's a good idea?" Amy asked me, her eyes wide. "I mean, Jake won't hit him or anything, will he?"

"Of course not," I reassured her, though I wasn't so sure myself.

The back door slammed. Libby marched through the kitchen, red-faced and pouting, and headed straight for the first-floor bathroom Pa had added just the year before. I would have bet a dollar she'd been out back with Dave and her father had sent her in the house. Libby idolized her Uncle Dave, and even though he was eight years older, she defended him like a she-bear with a cub. "He's got a lot of good inside him, Mom. He just needs someone to give him a chance."

It did no good at all to tell her he'd had more than his share of chances. She would just shake her head and assume a superior look that said, *You just don't understand.*

I didn't want to deal with that now.

I grabbed Anne's arm and hustled her into a corner behind

the stairs, where a small table held a telephone and a vase of plastic violets. Anne eased herself gratefully onto the polished wooden chair, while I tossed a throw pillow to the floor and settled down with relief.

Anne Marie smiled and closed her eyes. "Quite a crew, isn't it?"

I nodded. "With such a big family, Ma shouldn't ever feel alone."

Anne winced. "She will though. No one can fill a husband's space. No matter how hard they try. I mean, I still miss Frank, and he's been gone seven years. But Chuck does his best to try to keep my mind off it."

"You're still seeing each other then?"

"All the time. He's renting an apartment about six blocks from me. I think he's getting impatient." She looked deeply into my eyes. "He's softening, Celia, but until he comes to terms with his need for God, I can't marry him. Surely you understand that."

She was right, of course. My brother was a stubborn cuss, still insisting he could run his own life. He had changed a great deal from the furious, tormented young man who had attempted suicide. The accident he had caused on his stolen motorcycle had almost claimed both his and our uncle's lives. But because of it, our once-broken family had been reunited.

The last five years had not been easy for Chuck. He could not give up his hatred for the DuVals, who had adopted him and our sister Grace when they were little. Part of his resentment stemmed from the fact that they had renamed the baby Florence and insisted she was their natural child. Chuck was old enough to know the truth, and he never forgave them for their deception.

That my brother had fallen in love with Jake's sister was no mystery to me. Anne Marie was beautiful, inside and out. At thirty-seven she had kept her petite figure, and her soft dark hair didn't show a speck of gray. If she used Miss Clairol, no one could tell.

It was no secret that Chuck wanted to marry her. He had followed her back to San Francisco hoping they would become engaged. Neither of them seemed to mind that she was six years older. He agreed that her faith in God was part of what drew him to her, yet he insisted that their relationship shouldn't hinge on his commitment to her God—or his lack of it. But to Anne Marie it was the most important hinge of all.

I was about to ask her how long she was staying, when Libby appeared looking sullen and defiant.

"There you are, Mother. Dad's been looking all over for you. Boy, is he a grump."

"Watch your tone, dear," I said, "and button your sweater before he sees you, or you'll find out what grumpy really is!"

"Mother!" she huffed, but obeyed.

Libby had worn the new wool skirt and matching cardigan Aunt Rose had given her for Christmas. It was a smart-looking outfit, but she filled the sweater out a bit too well. If dear Aunt Rose had seen her with the top three buttons undone, she'd have repossessed the outfit and bought Libby a high-neck blouse instead.

I accepted Anne Marie's smile as a vote of sympathy and followed my daughter into the kitchen, where I found Jake cutting a slab of apple pie. He looked tired but otherwise composed. Dave sat on the living-room sofa staring through the window, like a punished five-year-old who would rather be outside playing.

By now most of the visitors were gone. John had left awhile ago, with apologies, but he'd taken off all the time he could from work. Brian's fiancée, Pam, hovered hopefully by the front door, and I knew they'd be leaving soon as well. Amy and her husband had already headed back to their home in Orange. Sara June and Steven were leaving for Sacramento in the morning. I hoped Anne Marie would volunteer to stay awhile longer, but I didn't want to ask her.

Jake chewed a mouthful of pie and offered me a bite. I shook my head. My stomach rebelled at the thought of more food.

He shrugged, finished the piece himself and set the plate down in the sink. "Are you ready, Celia? I'm beat, and I have to get back to the shop tomorrow. I promised Ron the day off."

I looked around the cluttered kitchen and felt suddenly exhausted. "Look at this mess. I should stay and help."

"Never mind that." Ma Freeman shuffled to the back porch with a load of paper plates and shoved them into the trash can. "You've both done enough. Anne and Sara will help me with the dishes. My boy needs his rest." She wrapped Jake in a tight hug, and I watched him struggle to control his tears. I didn't even try to stop my own as she hugged me too and urged us toward the door. "Don't forget your coats. It's turned cold again.

"My baby girl." She kissed Libby's forehead, then pushed her to arm's length and looked her in the eye. "Your grandpa loved you, Libby Jane. He was danged proud of you too, don't you ever forget that."

"I won't, Grandma," Libby promised, and fled through the front door.

Ten minutes later we finished our goodbys and headed for the car. Libby was standing by the curb next to Dave, talking to a young man on a motorcycle. He was dark with wavy hair, black boots and a black leather jacket identical to the one that Dave practically lived in. My heart thumped queerly. Jake honked the horn. Libby turned around, and I beckoned her to come. She mumbled something to Dave and his friend, then walked slowly down the sidewalk to the car and settled herself in the back seat.

"Who was that?" I asked her.

"You mean Miguel? He's no one. Just a friend of Uncle Dave's."

She sounded so nonchalant, but I could see her in the rear-view mirror, primping her hair and smirking like a cat lapping cream.

Chapter
Four

It was midnight before I thought to ask Jake about his conversation with the Freemans' pastor. By then he was sound asleep, and I promptly forgot all about it again.

On Wednesday morning Aunt Rose showed up with a pot of homemade soup. By the time we dropped Libby off at school and got over to Ma's, it was half past ten.

Ma Freeman was still running on nerves. Her eyes were swollen-red, but she greeted us like long-lost kin and poured the soup into a pan to heat for lunch. "Rose, dear, how sweet of you to think of us. Anne Marie loves chicken soup, and it does smell good."

Aunt Rose just smiled and drew her into the living room for "a nice long chat," which left Anne and me on our own.

"How's Florence, Celia?" Anne asked. "Chuck never talks about her. I think he's still smarting some from that scene at her wedding."

I winced. Our sister had married Jerry Fuller in August 1958, right after they both graduated with honors from the University of Southern California. She had invited both Chuck and me to the wedding, but I'd never imagined Chuck would go. I'd had to practically drag Jake by the ankles, and when we arrived, about fifteen minutes before the ceremony, Chuck wasn't there.

"We'll kiss the bride and go," I promised Jake when the service was over.

"I'll tell you what," he grinned, "you wait in line to kiss the bride while I go grab a piece of cake."

Poor Jake. He never did get any cake. We ran the gauntlet, as he put it: kissed Flo, congratulated Jerry and shook hands with the DuVals, who pretended we were strangers. We were just heading for the buffet when I heard a commotion behind us.

"Uh-oh. Look who just walked in." Jake wasn't smiling.

In fact no one was smiling. Except Chuck, but it was a sick smile, sick and sad, like at a funeral when you're trying to be brave and not break down so as not to upset the grieving family. Dr. DuVal's face was the color of molten lava. He had a good-size hunk of Chuck's shirt front clutched in one fist and looked ready to hit him with the other. Thank God, Chuck kept his own arms at his sides.

I still don't know exactly what was said, but Mrs. DuVal burst into tears. Flo handed her bouquet to the maid of honor, stamped her foot and bellowed, "Stop it!" at the top of her lungs. She grabbed her father's arm and held on until he let Chuck go. Then she glared hard at both men. "I will not allow you to ruin my wedding. If you can't behave like civilized adults, you can leave right now." She looked straight at Robert DuVal.

It was over as fast as it had begun. Jake took my arm when I tried to run to Chuck. "Better leave it, Celia. I'm sure we'll see him at the house tonight."

But Jake had been wrong. Chuck had headed straight back to San Francisco without so much as a hello to the rest of us.

"He was so embarrassed." Anne's comment told me she'd been remembering the whole thing too. "He really didn't intended to cause a scene. And I know he still loves his sister. They exchange letters, and they talk on the phone every few months."

I nodded. "Florence says only good things about him to me. I know she still loves him. But she loves her parents too, and it's hard on her to be in the middle like that. I wish ... Ah well, maybe someday it will settle. I guess it's best that Chuck's so far away." I squeezed Anne's hand and got up to call the others in to lunch.

"How long are you staying, Anne?" Aunt Rose broached the question I'd been dying to ask.

Anne looked at her mother. "I have to leave Sunday afternoon. The hospital's short-handed as it is, and I have to work a second shift all next week."

Aunt Rose looked disappointed. I knew she was lonely. She'd managed to keep a houseful most of the time since my cousin Billy was killed. During the war she had entertained airmen from the nearby army base. After the accident she had her hands full with Uncle Edward and Chuck. When Anne Marie moved in to help with the invalids, Aunt Rose was in her element. Mary Margaret, Jake, Libby and I were always in and out as well. I was afraid it would all be too much for her, but playing hostess to a large family—extended or real—was her delight.

Now, with Chuck and Anne living in San Francisco and Mary Margaret down south in San Diego, their visits were few and far between. Even Jake and I didn't make it down quite as often as we had when Libby was little. But if Aunt Rose felt deserted by her loved ones, she never complained.

Now she took Ma Freeman's hand. "If you need a change, Ella, please come and stay with us. It's still quiet enough where we are, and you'd be surprised how much the country air revives the soul."

Ma looked startled. "Well, thank you, Rose, but I'll be fine.

I have my home, and Davy still needs me to do for him."

Anne Marie looked miserable.

"Don't worry," I whispered as Aunt Rose and I climbed into the car to leave. "Jake and I will look after your mother—and Dave." She caught my meaning and flashed me a relieved smile.

* * *

Jake's mother sorted through Pa's things herself. "It's a comfort to me to handle them," she insisted. But one Saturday she called to ask if we could come fetch a bag of clothes for the missions closet. "Our church don't have one," she explained, "and I know First Baptist does."

"Every Saturday night Delbert would polish up his shoes," Ma confided as she handed Jake two paper bags. "Then he'd brush off his good blue suit and choose a tie to go with that ratty white shirt. I turned the collar on it once and made new cuffs, but it was an eyesore. I'd have bought him a new one out of the household money, but he wouldn't budge.

" 'The good Lord puts up with me from Monday to Saturday,' he'd say, 'so the least I can do is dress up for him on Sunday. But I'll be hanged if I'll spend hard-earned money on a new shirt when this one's got a button left to fasten it.' "

She shook her head. "He wasn't a mean man, but he was stubborn as a well-fed mule."

Jake loaded the bags into the trunk of the Chevy and came back into the house with his toolbox. "I'm going to fix that back door," he muttered and headed for the service porch.

"Land, you boys will spoil me!" Ma's face flushed with gratitude. "Brian came out last Sunday and mowed the lawn. I told him it weren't growin' much right now, but he said the weeds was high out back." She frowned. "I just don't get to the yard like I used to. Seems like there's always something needs doing in here." We both looked around the spacious kitchen. It was spotlessly clean, but the linoleum was popping up around the seams, the enamel sink had rusted almost through, and the oven door had to be propped shut with half a broom handle.

I knew Jake's father hadn't meant to let things go. He had been a hard worker who spent his life doing wiring and construction for other people. He just never seemed to keep up with his own.

The back door opened and shut smoothly, without a squeak. I watched through the window as Jake put his tool kit away, closed the car trunk and stood, hands shoved in his pockets, staring into space.

"How's my boy doing?"

Startled, I stepped back from the window. I hadn't realized Ma was watching too. "He's sad," I said finally, "like the rest of us. It will take awhile."

She nodded and moved to lift the boiling teakettle from the stove. She poured the water into three brown porcelain cups and stirred in instant Sanka. When she turned to set them on the table, she looked every one of her sixty-two years.

* * *

Jake pulled onto the freeway. "I don't like the thought of Ma being all alone in that big old house," he said once we were settled in the right-hand lane. "Maybe we could find her a small apartment."

"We could try, darling, but I don't think she wants to move."

Jake frowned. "Why in blazes not? She's lived in that shabby old cave for forty years. You'd think she'd want something new for a change."

Jake's grief had taken on the form of anger. I had to remind myself, and Libby too, that it would pass. At least I hoped it would. Grief could turn a person inside out and backwards. Just look at what it did to Mama. "It's her home, Jake," I said quietly. "Full of memories. I think we should let her be awhile."

He didn't say anything more until we pulled into the driveway. Then he turned and laid his arm along the back of the seat, like he used to do before we were married. "You know, it's funny," he said. "Their pastor told me at the funeral that Pa had left some money. He gave me a note in Pa's hand that said who was to get what. But doggone it, Celia, even with social security there's barely enough for Ma to live on. How could he expect us to take a share?"

I was as puzzled as Jake. His folks had never had any money. Raising eight kids had taken its toll on their pocketbook as well as the house. How could Pa have left anything behind? "Maybe there's a bank account?"

Jake laughed. "Are you kidding? Pa wouldn't go near a bank after the thirties. Didn't trust them at all. Come to think of it, Pa didn't trust anyone where money was concerned. If one of us kids needed something, he'd send us to our room, then go off awhile and come back with some cash. We had to keep an account of every penny, and Lord help us if we didn't bring back the change.

"He was the same with Ma. She got her household money in an envelope at the beginning of every month. If it ran out . . ." He shrugged. "Well, we made do." His mouth twisted in a smile. "But it got so I hated pork and beans."

It was getting cold in the car, but Jake made no move to open the door. I finally broke the silence. "Have you mentioned anything about the money to the others? They've been there longer than you—maybe John or Brian . . . ?"

Jake shook his head. "They would have said something. Besides, the pastor said Pa had confided in him alone. Pa made the man promise to tell no one but me."

When I thought about it, I guessed that made sense to a man like Pa. The Freemans had attended Westside Presbyterian for years. Who better to trust your secrets to than a man of God?

Jake sighed and opened the car door. "Ah well, it really

doesn't matter, does it? Ma's the one entitled to anything that's left." His head snapped back around. "And don't you say anything. If Dave got wind there was any money at all, he'd badger Ma to death."

His words stung. *He's still grieving,* I told myself. *He doesn't realize what he's saying.*

"Oh, I forgot to tell you," he said, fumbling with the latch on the door. "I gave Dave a job as a grease monkey. He starts work tomorrow. If he keeps his nose clean, he just might make a passable mechanic."

Jake and his employee, Ron, had a good relationship. They went fishing together and once in a while took in a ball game. Jake was always saying how Ron was a hard worker. "He's a big help to me. If anyone deserves a few bonuses or an extra day off, it's him."

But the thought of Dave working for Jake gnawed on my mind like a dog worrying a bone. They couldn't be in the same room for two minutes without wanting to cut each other's throat. How on earth would they be able to work together?

Chapter
Five

Toward the end of the month, Green Bay won the pro football championships, John Fitzgerald Kennedy became president of the United States, and NASA sent a poor helpless chimpanzee into space.

Jake and I had gone over to Sam and Dotty's as usual so the boys could watch the game on television and Dot and I could catch up on each other's lives. I talked to her at least three times a week on the telephone, but with her six kids and all the things going on with our family, we never ran out of conversation. Besides, we hadn't really gotten together since Pa died.

The guys were in the den hooting and hollering over the game, while Dot and I sat on the sofa in the living room trying to talk and at the same time corral her youngest son, Mikey.

"Did you read about them sending that monkey into orbit?" I asked Dotty. "How can they treat an animal like that? What if something goes wrong? The capsule could blow up, or he could die of starvation."

"That's why they sent a chimp, Celia. They're testing the equipment. The Russians have already sent two men into space. You can mark my words, we're next." She glanced away. "Jonathan Michael! You let go of that cat's tail." She grabbed for

Mikey's shirttail, but he just grinned and scooted out of reach. Dotty sighed. "He'll be the death of me yet, and that poor cat has already lost eight lives. If you ask me, it's in more danger than that chimpanzee."

I smiled. Mikey was not quite four, and a holy terror. He was Dot and Sam's surprise baby, a good six years younger than his closest brother, Zeke. Dotty had been thirty-two when he was born, and she had aged a great deal since.

"Six kids would give anyone gray hair," Jake said. I agreed, but I also knew that neither Dot nor Sam would have traded any one of them. For that matter, neither would we.

The oldest, Rachel, was a sweet fifteen, popular, outgoing and Libby's best friend. They were in Glee Club together and still took skating lessons at the roller rink on Saturday afternoons. They giggled over boys, and both thought Elvis Presley was "cool." As soon as we'd arrived, they had scrambled up to Rachel's room to listen to some "boss" disk jockey called Wolfman Jack.

The oldest boy, David, was in his room. "He's reading *A Tale of Two Cities* for English class," Dotty confided, "and he's actually enjoying it!"

I laughed. David had been almost as wild as Mikey when he was little. Now, at fourteen, he was the scholar of the bunch. He had inherited Sam's dark good looks and slender frame. He lived with his nose in a book, and Sam swore he had a penchant for the law. David just smiled at his father's predictions for his future and kept his views on the subject to himself.

The front door opened, and two mud-caked heads peered around the door frame. "Mom? Can we have a towel?"

Dotty gasped. "A towel? You need a water hose! Where have you two been?"

Two sets of ivory-white teeth appeared beneath the cracking brown masks. "Playing football," the twins piped in unison.

I laughed. Sarah and J. Joe were precocious twelve-year-olds and inseparable. Up till now, Sarah had easily assumed the role of tomboy. "Don't worry about it," I said to Dotty after she sent them around to the back porch to change. "She's almost thirteen. I bet you'll see another side to her soon."

"I hope so," Dotty said, "and so does their teacher. Last week at recess she ordered J. Joe to play baseball with the boys, which was fine with him, but she had a mutiny on her hands when Sarah discovered she wasn't allowed to join them. J. Joe refused to pick up a bat, and Sarah wound up in the office when she kicked the third baseman in the shins."

I started to laugh, and Dotty joined in. "It's funny now, but it wasn't then. When the principal asked Sarah why she'd done such a horrid thing, she looked her straight in the eye and said, 'He called J. a sissy. No one calls my brother a sissy.' "

Dotty sighed and made another grab for Mikey, who was tormenting the cat again. The cat managed to escape and bounded to a precarious perch on the windowsill. But Mikey wasn't ready to give up. He squeezed between Sam's recliner and the lamp table and was within inches of capturing the twitching tail when Dotty caught him and smacked his behind.

"What's going on in here?" Sam appeared in the doorway with a bottle of Coke in one hand and a bologna sandwich in the other.

"Your son is intent on murdering the cat, as usual." Dotty pushed the squirming youngster toward his father. "Here, why don't you take over for a while?"

"Sure." Sam swallowed the remains of his sandwich, handed the Coke to Mikey and scooped him up onto his shoulders. He paused for a moment to balance his load, then limped toward the door. "Come on, tiger, it's halftime. Let's go watch the pretty girls."

Mikey grinned, like he knew exactly what his father meant,

and downed the rest of the soft drink in one gulp. Sam set him down in the doorway and shooed him on down the hall.

"You girls had better eat, if you're going to. Jake is on his third sandwich, and Zeke's not far behind."

I smiled. Ezekiel had always been "little Zeke" to us, although he was starting to resent it. He'd been the baby of the bunch until Mikey came along. Now, at ten, he was calmer than he'd been at four, but just as good-natured. "If Zeke isn't smiling," Dotty said once, "I take his temperature."

I waited until I heard the door to the den open and close, then turned to Dotty. "Are Sam's legs worse, or is it just my imagination?"

Dotty stared at the empty doorway. "The left one bothers him more and more. The doctor says there's arthritis in the joints. There's not much they can do. Except for drugs, of course. And Sam won't take anything stronger than aspirin."

I nodded. It had been over twenty years since the hit-and-run that had mangled Sam's legs and left him crippled. It was a miracle he could walk at all. The doctors had been amazed when the feeling returned to both legs and he was able to learn to walk again. Even they had to give the credit where it belonged. "This is impossible," the surgeon had insisted. "It has to be an act of God." We agreed, of course.

"The other night," Dotty continued, still studying the empty doorway, "he told me he welcomes the pain because it keeps him on the edge. When I asked him what he meant, he said, 'It reminds me why I work so hard to fight for justice in the courts. The more criminals I can put behind bars, the fewer victims will have to suffer.' "

She shook her head. "Sam's ecstatic that President Kennedy has appointed his brother Robert as the new attorney general. He says the man will stop at nothing to fight organized crime. Sam would give his eyeteeth to be a part of it."

I shivered. The gangsters who were responsible for my papa's death in 1936, and who later attacked Sam and me, had been caught and put in prison a long time ago. Yet I still had nightmares about them once in a while. Sam lived with the effects of it every day of his life.

I was still thinking about it when Jake and I got home.

"Sam's really enthusiastic about this administration," Jake said when I repeated what Dot had told me. "He thinks Kennedy will keep both the criminals and the commies in line." He finished locking the doors and followed me into the bedroom. "Sam told me today a friend on the Supreme Court has recommended him to Robert Kennedy for a staff position."

"A staff position?" I sat straight up in bed. "You mean, Sam might go to work for the attorney general of the United States?"

The mattress squeaked as Jake climbed in beside me and pulled me close. "The key word is *might,* Celia. Sam's a brilliant lawyer, but not really a politician, and there's lots of competition for those positions."

I rested my head on my husband's shoulder. "But wouldn't he have to live in Washington then?"

"Didn't I tell you not to worry about it? It's not likely to happen."

But even after Jake kissed me good night and rolled over on his other side. I lay awake, feeling uneasy. It was selfish, I knew, but if Sam and Dotty moved to Washington, I'd be losing my best friend.

Chapter Six

I hadn't heard from my cousin Mary Margaret in months. Libby still got letters, and Aunt Rose kept in touch with a once-a-week phone call, but ever since Jake and I had suggested to M that her lifestyle might be a bad influence on Libby, she hadn't had much to say to either of us.

We were all dumbfounded when she quit her job at Douglas in 1956, packed up lock, stock and barrel, and moved to San Diego. Her latest boyfriend drove her down in his pickup truck, got her settled in a one-bedroom duplex, then came back to Los Angeles and married someone else. Instead of being devastated, Mary Margaret put on her three-inch heels and a little black cocktail dress and found a job as hostess at a ritzy dinner house. Then she marched into the administration office at San Diego State and registered for the first term of a four-year degree in accounting. At thirty-six years old!

The only one not surprised was Uncle Edward. "Mary Margaret has always been smart," he said. "She may not have much sense when it comes to men, but she's too intelligent to waste her mind on the assembly line at an aircraft plant. She may have made more money at Douglas, but in the long run I think it'll be the best move she could have made."

Aunt Rose agreed. "Our girl has always had a good head on her shoulders. One of these days she'll get it connected to her heart."

The truth was, Mary Margaret had made a bad mistake when she married Wesley Harris at seventeen. He was a womanizer who never really loved anyone but himself. Nonetheless, their divorce devastated her. But instead of turning to God for answers, she turned to a succession of men, and she was genuinely surprised when none of them turned out to be her one true love. In the last few years she had set her love life aside to concentrate on her career.

When we saw her at Christmastime, she had seemed happy but more subdued. Even Libby commented on it. "Aunt M must have had a headache today," she told us. "She hardly said a word at dinner, and when I asked her what movie she had seen last, she said, 'I rarely go to movies anymore.' Wow, is she losing it!"

Jake snorted. "Ha! Don't tell her that! For once in her life she's acting her age."

I hid my smile. "All right, you two. Mary Margaret is a businesswoman now. She has to dress and act conservatively. It's bound to affect her everyday life as well." It was true. After a couple of entry-level jobs, M had finally landed a position with Willow and Wall, a prominent accounting firm in La Mirada. I was proud of her, and I think Jake was too. But it would take more than a business suit and refined dinner conversation to convince him she had settled down.

"Right," he countered. "And pigs fly."

"Daddy, stop! You're always picking on Aunt M. Tell him to stop it, Mother, he's not being fair."

I took a deep breath and stepped in before Jake could make it worse. "Watch your tone, Libby." My own tone must have been convincing. Libby settled back in her seat without a backsass, and Jake kept his rebuttal to himself.

I sighed. Scenes like this were exactly what drove Jake to distraction where my cousin was concerned. He and Libby had been at loggerheads since she hit puberty, and Jake had it in his head to blame Mary Margaret. I tried to tell him that girls Libby's age will act up with or without any help from someone else, but he had convinced himself that the source of Libby's rebellion was "that loose-living cousin of yours." I was beginning to think nothing this side of eternity would change his mind.

We didn't hear from Mary Margaret again until January, when she sent a note through Libby. "Jake, I was saddened to hear about the death of your father, please give my condolences to your mother and the rest of the family. Love, M."

Then on the morning of May 1, 1961, I got a phone call.

"Celia, it's M. I'm in L.A. on business, and I wondered if we could have lunch."

I tried not to sound shocked. "Today? Well, of course . . . I mean, I did have plans, but if you're only here one day . . ."

That meant I would have to cancel lunch with my sister and our friend Stuart Haley. I had met Stuart in 1956 when I ventured onto the USC campus to track down Florence. In spite of the fact that Robert DuVal had warned us to stay away from her, I had felt we needed to meet and talk. So I gathered my courage and went to the school, thinking I could just run into her. But I hadn't realized the campus would be so big. I was about to give it up and go home when a tall, good-looking man literally popped out of the bushes and took me straight to Flo. It turned out he was an English professor and was working on a Ph.D. in psychology besides.

Mary Margaret interrupted my thoughts. "It's important, Celia, or I wouldn't ask."

I tried to picture what was in the fridge and cupboards. "Would you like to come here? I can fix some sandwiches or something."

"No. I think we should meet on neutral ground. How about the Central Café? It's only a few blocks from your office. I can take a cab from my hotel. Check-out is at eleven, so shall we say eleven-thirty?"

I wanted to drop the phone like a hot potato and pretend she hadn't called. Instead I heard myself say, "Fine, I'll see you then."

Uncle Edward told me once, "When you have a problem, face it head-on. If you turn and run, sooner or later it will catch up with you, and you'll find it's even bigger than before."

I hung up and dialed Stuart's office at the university.

Stuart and I had had lunch many times over the years—always with Flo and Jerry, of course. After they were married, Flo stayed on as a graduate student while Jerry landed a job designing houses for the rich and famous in Beverly Hills. Now she was just a year away from her own dream of teaching art history at the college level. Stuart had hinted more than once that he was sure there'd be a position for her right there at USC.

Over time, Stuart and I became good friends. He had a listening ear and a way of giving well-thought-out advice without sounding like a know-it-all. We'd had him to dinner once or twice, and Jake liked him well enough, but the campus was only a few blocks from the Children's Charities office where I worked; it was easier just to get together with him and Flo on my lunch hour.

It took awhile for Stuart to pick up the phone. I was about to call the administration office and ask them to deliver a message to Florence, when he answered on the eighth ring.

"I'm sorry, too," he said when I explained. "Florence will be disappointed, but I'm sure she'll understand." He hesitated, then added, "How about next week? Florence has some news she wants to share."

—42—

I promised to meet them on Monday, hung up and realized with dismay that I'd missed my bus. "Oh, drat," I said aloud. "Now I'll have to drive."

* * *

I was half an hour late for work and had to park in the lot six blocks away. Mr. Johnson was in conference with some people from the county, so I decided to get yesterday's reports filed away. I managed to pop a run in my nylon on the file cabinet drawer and bruise my leg besides.

At 11:15 I closed the file on a three-month-old infant who needed temporary foster care while his mother was in jail. I penciled a note on the cover saying I thought the baby would do well with Mrs. Garcia, an older woman with three school-age children. She loved babies, and the ones we had placed in her care so far had done well.

I fished my purse out of the bottom desk drawer and went in to tell Mr. Johnson I was going to lunch. Instead of saying, "Have a good lunch, Celia, and thanks for your work," like he always did, he stood up and motioned to the padded armchair in front of his desk.

"Please sit down a minute. I have to talk to you." He fidgeted with the collar of his shirt, pulling it away from his neck and straightening his tie. His face took on a queer blue-red color, and for a minute I thought he was choking. But he cleared his throat and sank into his swivel chair.

"Celia, as you know, the minimum wage has gone up to $1.25 an hour. Goodness knows, you deserve that—and a lot more— but the sad news is we're on a limited budget, and we have to hire two new social workers." He picked up a pencil, tapped the blotter three times and slammed it down again. "That means," he huffed, "not only can we not afford your raise, but we have to let you go."

I was stunned. I'd grown to love this job over the years. Not only did it give me a chance to use my secretarial skills, but it allowed me to help children as well. I had come to feel that each child placed into a loving home was another gold piece added to heaven's treasure.

Oh, my part was small enough. All I did was evaluate some of the cases, make recommendations for foster homes, and type up the paperwork. It was Mr. Johnson and the board who made the final decisions. But I felt as if I knew the children personally, and I prayed for them every day.

Mr. Johnson came around to my side of the desk and put his arm around my shoulder in a fatherly hug. "Doggone it, Celia, I hate like crazy to see you go. You're the best thing that's happened to this program in years. If it were up to me, you'd be promoted. But the fact is, you don't have a degree. It's out of my hands."

I nodded mechanically, afraid I might start to cry. "I'll just get my things," I stammered, then looked at the clock. "Oh dear, I'm late and Mary Margaret's waiting. May I—?"

"Of course. Come back for your things anytime. Celia, I'm sorry."

He looked like he was about to cry, and I just couldn't face that right then. I ran out of the office, kicked off my shoes and ran two blocks to the Central Café in my stocking feet, carrying my purse and a pair of two-inch cherry-red high heels.

Chapter
Seven

Later that month, Alan Shepard was the first American in space. But when Jake heard what Mary Margaret had to say, I thought he would beat him to it.

She'd been sweet as pie at first. "How are you, Celia? And how's Jake's mother doing? I know what it's like to lose a husband. She must be pretty lonely after all those years. Oh, and by the way, I think you and Jake need to pay more attention to your daughter."

That's not exactly how it went, of course, but it seemed like a bolt out of the blue, and I was in no mood to coddle one of Mary Margaret's flights of fantasy. When Libby was small, my cousin had accused us of being overprotective: "How will she ever learn to cope if you don't let her fall once in a while?" When she got older, we were accused of being too strict: "Let her live a little. If you box up a mouse, it will just chew its way out and get swallowed by the cat." Now it appeared we weren't being protective or strict enough.

"What in the world is it now?" I had just caught my breath from my two-block run and took a long drink of my Coke.

"Well." She set her coffee cup back on the table and turned sideways in her chair, casually crossing one leg over the other in a nonchalant pose. "I got a letter last week from Liberty Jane. As much as I hate to betray her confidence, I thought you should know that, while you and Jake are at work—or doing whatever it is you do with your spare time—Libby is chasing around town with a bunch of beer-drinking motorcycle thugs."

I must have turned six shades of pale. The waitress rushed over to ask if there was something wrong with my sandwich and did I need another glass of water. And Mary Margaret just sat there waiting for the shock to run its course.

Once I saw a magic act where a man yanked the cloth from under fine bone china on a table. The dishes barely wiggled, but the audience held its breath for twenty seconds after. Then we all burst into applause. I was breathless now, but I sure didn't feel like applauding. Mary Margaret was no crowd-pleaser.

She wouldn't give me details, but apparently Libby had bragged about dating one of her Uncle Dave's friends, drinking her first beer and riding down Hollywood Boulevard on the back of his motorcycle.

My cousin delivered the punch line, then looked at her watch. "Oh dear, I've got to run. I'm sorry, Celia. Teenagers can be a handful, but I'm sure it's just a phase." She patted my arm, then picked up the check. "This one's on me. Let me know if there's anything I can do."

"No thank you, Mary Margaret, you've done enough," I said, but she was already halfway to the door.

*　*　*

We confronted Libby, of course. We didn't tell her that the information came from Mary Margaret; we just said that someone had seen her breaking the rules and wondered what she had to say for herself.

She denied everything at first. Then, between fits of outrage and tears of remorse, she confessed that yes, she had gone riding with one of Uncle Dave's friends and had some beer.

"But it was only a sip or two. And Miguel is nice. He's a lot younger than Uncle Dave and a real safe driver."

Jake looked like he needed two trips around the moon to cool off, so I sent Libby to her room. "We're not through with this, young lady. Your father and I need to talk about your punishment."

"Punishment! I am sixteen years old. You can't treat me like a baby!" She screamed like we'd beat her with a hickory stick. That possibility must have occurred to her as well when she saw her father's face. She spun on her heels and ran into her room without any more sass.

Jake slammed out of the house, jumped into the car and took the corner at Lafayette on two wheels. When he came back an hour later, he was more composed.

"I won't have it, Celia. She knows the rules about motorcycles, not to mention beer. And I will not have her running with a spic!"

"Jake! That sounds awful. I've never known you to be prejudiced."

"Prejudiced? I'm not prejudiced. Anyway, that's got nothing to do with it. The kid's a juvenile delinquent."

I held my hand up before he could sound off again. "I agree. We certainly don't want her involved with someone from that gang of hoodlums."

Jake swallowed the last of his coffee and flipped on the TV. "Well, just make sure she understands that. And no dates at all until she can behave. No daughter of mine is going to be branded as a hussy." He switched to channel 5, where Marshall Matt Dillon was bringing his unique brand of justice to Dodge City. Jake watched a minute, then continued. "I'll have a talk with Dave tomorrow—if the lazy bum shows up for work, that is. He's the one who introduced them; he can see to it that the creep stays away from her."

Libby refused to come out of her room for dinner, so I let her be. Jake turned off the television and headed for bed at nine.

It had been an exhausting day. I had taken two aspirins for the headache pounding at my temples, but they hadn't helped a bit. I would have given anything to follow Jake and sleep the pain away, but I knew I couldn't let my talk with Libby go until morning. "Never let the sun go down on your wrath," the Bible said, and I knew it was good advice. Going to bed on trouble only caused it to multiply. So even though it was the middle of spring and seventy-five degrees outside, I fixed a cup of Libby's favorite cocoa, with the tiny marshmallows she liked so well, and tapped on her bedroom door.

I heard the sheets rustle and the radio click off. "Come in." Her voice was gravelly, and her eyes were red from crying. She lowered them to the book on her lap when I crossed to the side of her bed and set the cocoa on the table. She was supposed to be doing homework, not reading a novel, but I let that slide.

I sat down on the bedspread. "Libby, honey, Daddy and I don't make rules to spoil your fun. We just want you to be safe and happy."

"But Mom," she blurted, "I'm happy when I'm with Miguel. And safe. Uncle Dave rides motorcycles all the time, so does Uncle Chuck, and they never get hurt." The minute she said it, she knew she'd been had. She blushed and tried to blunder on through. "That accident with Uncle Edward was different," she stammered. "Uncle Chuck was drinking and he wasn't being careful." She must have realized that she was only making matters worse.

"Anyway," she changed the subject, "Miguel is cool. He's nice, Mom, and so mature. Not like the boys at school. You'll like him. I could bring him over for dinner. I would have let you meet him before, but I knew Daddy would flip out because Miguel's a friend of Dave's."

I didn't bother to say that *flip out* was a mild term for what Jake would do if she brought Miguel home. I did explain our reasons for wanting her to date Christian boys her own age and race. "Your cultures and beliefs are just too different," I finished.

I could tell by the fire in her eyes that she had a comeback brewing, and I suddenly felt weary beyond belief. "No more, Libby. We've all had a hard day." I kissed her forehead and moved toward the door. "Your father and I have decided no dates for two weeks. And then we have to know exactly where you're going and we want to meet the boy." I opened the door, expecting a stream of protest. When there was none, I continued. "No more motorcycles, Libby. And no more beer. Is that clear?"

"Yes, Mother." Her tone would have frozen fire, but I was much too tired to care.

Chapter
Eight

I cleaned out my desk at Children's Charities and said goodby
to Mr. Johnson and the rest of the staff. Mr. Johnson looked
glum. He presented me with a coffee mug that had "World's
Greatest Secretary" plastered across the front in bold blue letters. Then two of the social workers came in with a box of
caramels and a single yellow rose. "We'll miss you, Celia," they
said. "You helped us and the children more than you'll ever
know."

By the time I had everything arranged in the bag I'd got
when I bought Libby's bedspread at the May Co., they had me
sniffling and remembering every goodby I'd ever said. Truth to
tell, I never did like changes. Even when they ended up turning
out for the better, they always were painful at the start.

* * *

I had to stop at the rest room to repair my face, which made
me five minutes late for lunch. But this time I kept my shoes
on and forced myself to walk at a casual pace. I was meeting
my sister and Stuart at the Central Café—the same place I'd
met Mary Margaret. And I was determined not to look flustered.

When I walked in, they were already seated, with coffee and

sandwich menus in hand. I knew Stuart had a class right after lunch, so I was glad they'd started without me.

"Celia," Stuart stood and pulled out my chair, "it's good to see you." He squeezed my hand, and I leaned over to kiss Flo's cheek.

"It's good to see you both. I'm sorry about last week."

Stuart gave me a curious look. Flo smiled and went back to her menu. I was glad they both let it go. I didn't feel like explaining about Libby just then.

After the waitress had taken our order, Stuart grinned and looked smugly at Flo. "Well, Florence, aren't you going to tell your sister the good news?"

"That's right," I said, "Stuart did say you had something to tell me." My hand flew to my mouth. "Oh, Flo, are you—?"

Florence looked stunned, then she laughed out loud. "No, Celia, I'm not . . . expecting, if that's what you mean." Her eyes gleamed wickedly, and I blushed. Stuart chuckled and took a bite of the hamburger the waitress had just set in front of him.

"Anyway, Jerry and I don't really want a family for a while, because"—she paused for effect—"I just got a teaching job for next fall. Right here at USC. Stuart put in a good word for me with the administration board." She cast him a grateful smile.

"Oh, Flo, that's wonderful! Stuart, how thoughtful. I know she'll do a fine job."

"So do I, or I wouldn't have recommended her." He smiled fondly at his former student, then turned his attention back to me. "The opening came up and the board made their decision last week. We were going to tell you, but you so cruelly broke our luncheon date."

His tone was light, like a cat batting water and hoping he might snag a goldfish. I decided to give him just a nibble.

"I'm sorry. My cousin came in unexpectedly from San Diego, and she only had one day."

Florence shrugged. "Don't worry about it, sis. What's in the bag?"

Grateful for the change of subject, I explained what had happened at Children's Charities. "So I am currently unemployed."

"What did Jake say?"

"Actually, I think he was glad. He wants me home more." I started to say "with Libby," but Libby was a subject I wanted to avoid.

Stuart looked thoughtful. "I'm sorry, Celia. I know how much that job meant to you."

I nodded and, to my dismay, realized I was about to cry again.

He patted my hand. "It would be easy to get caught up with the children. Some of those cases can be devastating. It must have been rewarding to know you were able to really help some of them."

When we finished lunch, Stuart picked up the tab and ushered Flo and me out of the restaurant. By the time I stood at the bus stop and watched them walk back toward the campus, I felt better. All the way home I basked in the glow of Flo's success and Stuart's understanding.

* * *

Jake called at six and said he'd be a couple hours late. "I'm sorry, babe. I can't talk about it now, but something's come up and I have to get it settled. I'll be home as soon as I can."

He sounded weary and sad, as if the whole world had gone to pieces and left him to clean up the mess. And I guess it had. His world, anyway. With his father gone, I knew he felt responsible for his mother and his brother Dave, as well as Libby and me. Libby's little escapade hadn't helped. And the fact that Mary Margaret had brought it to our attention galled him even more.

"Talk about the pot calling the kettle black," Jake had fumed.

"Look at the influence she's had on Libby. With all the shenanigans your cousin's been up to, you'd think she'd be the last one to tell tales."

I tried to be the voice of reason. "Would you have wanted her to keep quiet? Lord only knows what kind of trouble Libby would have gotten into if Mary Margaret hadn't intervened. Aunt Rose says God used Mary Margaret to protect her, and as irritating as M can be, I have to say I agree with her."

Jake couldn't answer back to that. He just let his shoulders droop and crawled off to bed, leaving me feeling guilty for no good reason, and frustrated besides. I felt like spiders had spun a web of grief around me, trapping me in the middle like a fast-caught fly.

That day's lunch with Florence and Stuart had been a much-needed respite for me, and Jake's hint of further trouble left me feeling more resentful than afraid.

"Will there ever be an end?" I sighed to Dotty on the phone.

"Not until the good Lord takes us home. Relax, girl, and take one problem at a time."

I heard a car door slam. "Oh, grief. That must be Libby, back from the library. And Jake should be home any minute. I don't know how you handle seven of them."

Dotty laughed. "Six. No, five. Sam and Rachel are no trouble at all."

I hung up just as Libby stormed into the house. She dumped a load of books into Jake's recliner and turned on me with a glare that could have melted wax. "What did Daddy do to Uncle Dave?"

"Liberty Jane, your father hasn't done a thing to Uncle Dave." Then I remembered the "something to be settled" at the shop. My face must have given me away.

"Yes he has. Why else would Uncle Dave pack everything on his bike and take off for Mexico?"

"Mexico? Why on earth would Dave go to Mexico? And just where did you get all this information?"

Her face lost some of its defiance. She shrugged and studied the pattern in the carpet. "From Miguel."

"I thought we made it clear—"

Her head snapped up. "I had to tell him goodby, didn't I? It would have been rude to just break up with him and not tell him why. And no, I didn't ride on his bike or drink any beer."

Her sarcasm made me want to smack her. "Watch your tone, young lady. And pick up those books. Your father will be home any minute."

I was glad when she did as she was told and marched off to her room. I should have known that trouble at the shop meant Dave. He and Jake must have had a fight. I needed time to gather my wits and think—and maybe say a prayer or two—but I heard the sound of Jake's Impala pulling in the drive. He had just shut the garage door when the telephone rang.

It was Ma Freeman. She sounded excited and out of breath. "Celia, dear, I hate to bother you at this hour, but is my boy there? I need to talk to him."

"Hold on a minute, Ma, he just walked in the door."

I covered the mouthpiece with my hand. "Darling, it's your mother," I said. Then my heart dropped to my feet. "Jake!" I gasped. "What happened to you?"

He looked like he'd been run over by a garbage truck. His work shirt was torn and smeared with grease. He had a cut over one eye and bloodstains on his pants and shoes.

C h a p t e r
N i n e

Jake was not a big man, but he was strong and had been quite a scrapper in his younger days. He had a scar over one eye from when he'd knocked Roy Cummings in the gutter, and scars on his back and shoulder from Pearl. But war or no war, he hadn't been in a fight in years. I studied his head and face for any other signs of blood and was relieved to find none.

Jake took the telephone. He listened for a minute, then said, "All right, Ma. Just give me a minute to change, and we'll be right there."

Libby came out of her room and screamed when she saw her father. "Daddy! You're hurt!" She ran to him and threw her arms around his waist like a frightened two-year-old.

Jake looked astonished, but he hugged her and kissed the part in her hair. "I'm okay, sugar. It probably looks worse than it is." He looked at me over the top of her head. "I'd better go wash up. Ma needs me."

"Jake!"

"Daddy!"

He must have realized he wouldn't get a shower until he'd given us both an explanation. "Look, it's nothing really. Dave had his hand in the till once too often. I caught him red-handed and let him go. We were both upset, but neither of us was really hurt."

"You and Uncle Dave had a fight and you fired him? Daddy, how could you? He needed that job. Couldn't you have given him a second chance?"

"Now look here, Libby," Jake started, but she had already run into her room.

I could tell he'd reached his limit. "It's all right, darling, let it go. Nothing we say or do can please her right now." I took his hand, and he winced when I rubbed the bruised knuckles. "It's you I'm worried about. Let me call your mother and tell her you'll see her in the morning."

He sighed and touched my cheek with his free hand. His deep brown eyes had faded to a hazy gray. "No, I have to go. She's really upset, talking about some money and a will. I don't know what Dave's got to do with it, but he's disappeared again."

I nodded. "He's probably in Mexico by now." I could have bit my tongue in half.

"Mexico?" Jake looked at me like I'd just grown two heads, turned around and groped his way into the bathroom.

* * *

Ma Freeman blew her nose on a ragged linen handkerchief. "I know our Davy has been a trial in the past. But since poor Delbert's passing he's been a different boy. And such a help to me. I just can't understand what made him take off like that."

We were sitting in her living room, trying to figure out what was going on. It was like working a jigsaw puzzle with several pieces missing.

Jake sat on the edge of the slipcovered sofa, studying the letter his mother had handed him the minute we walked in the door. He scowled. "There were some problems at the shop," Jake told her, "and I had to let him go. He'll be back, Ma. He always comes back."

"I don't know," she said. "He's never took this much with him before. And he's seen the letter Pastor Riley brought by this morning. It said Dave wasn't to have his share of anything until he could prove himself responsible. He must've thought his pa didn't love him, but that's not true. Not true at all."

Jake looked up. "When did you say your pastor brought this letter?"

Ma sniffed. "This morning, right after Davy left for work. He didn't phone, just rang the doorbell. And there I was in that tattered old robe. I was so ashamed. Here it was almost eight o'clock and I wasn't dressed. But Pastor Riley didn't seem to care. 'I'm embarrassed myself,' he says, without even coming in. 'I thought I'd given Jake all the papers your husband left with me, but I found this one last night tucked between chapters 2 and 3 of Ecclesiastes in the old Bible he asked me to keep. Anyway, this was addressed to you, so I thought I'd better deliver it in person.'

"Well, when I read the letter, I'd have liked to died. I can't think where Delbert's mind was, hiding money in the yard. And in a well, he says, but we ain't got no well."

"Yes we do, Ma."

Jake pushed himself up, walked over to the phone and dialed a number.

"Jake, it's after ten o'clock."

He held up his hand. "Brian? Jake. Can you come over to Ma's tomorrow morning? I need your help with something. Six is fine. And bring John, if he can get away. Okay, thanks." He hung up the phone, came back to the sofa and put his arms around his mother.

"Ma, I promise you we'll straighten this out. But it's too late to do it now. If there really is some hidden cash, and if it's where I think it is, we'll need light and time to get it out." He straightened up slowly and rubbed his face with both hands. "Just promise me one thing."

Ma blinked up at him through her tears.

"Don't get your hopes up. Just because Pa hid money away doesn't mean it's still there."

He didn't say it, but I knew what he was thinking. If Dave had seen his father's note this afternoon, the money could very well be with him in Mexico.

* * *

The Freemans' property was once farmland, part of a large operation that had been sectioned off and sold in one- and two-acre parcels in the late 1920s. Delbert Freeman had bought this place in 1925. He'd tinkered with the house until he'd made it livable, dug his Ella a garden plot, built a lean-to for the Model A and let the rest, including the apple orchard on the very back of the property, go wild.

The letter Pa had written—"just in case I pass on first"—said there was money hidden in the well. And the only well within thirty miles was the one out where the orchard used to be. It had been boarded up before he'd bought the land. As far as anyone knew, he'd checked it only once to be sure none of his babies could fall in, then let it be.

"When we were kids," Jake related the next morning, "Tim and I used to play soldier out behind the house. We found the well one day and asked Pa if we could have the wooden cover for our fort. He said if we went near that old well again, we'd have to build a fort with plenty of standing room 'cause we wouldn't be able to sit for a year."

John laughed at Jake's imitation. "That sounds like Pa, all right." He pointed out the window. "The sun's up. Let's get to it." There was a gleam of adventure in his eye.

Jake took another gulp of coffee and pushed reluctantly to his feet. "Yeah, I guess we'd better get it over with.

"Celia, you and Ma stay here. The grass is tall out back.

There's sure to be snakes." His look said *Keep Ma busy,* but I
didn't need any incentive to stay away. I hated snakes as much
as I hated spiders; he couldn't have paid me to go back there.

Ma sighed. "Poor Delbert. His daddy never had a red cent.
They had a roof over their heads and beans in the pot and that
was all. Lord knows he never had a chance to get to know a
banker, let alone trust one. 'Hang on to your own purse,' Delbert's daddy told him. 'No sense in givin' some shifty no-ac-
count a chance to steal it.' The thirties proved him out. Pa
wouldn't have nothing to do with banks and loans and such. If
he put some aside for a rainy day, I guess he could have hid it
in a well."

I looked around the rundown house. It was spotlessly clean,
as usual, but no amount of scrubbing would ever restore it to
new. It had been old when they bought it. I thought about the
people it had sheltered, the children running barefoot across its
hardwood floors and carving notches on the newel post to mark
their height. The kitchen must have hosted a million meals, the
wooden stove warmed countless hands and feet. *Poor, tired old
house,* I thought, and started to cry.

Ma put her arms around me and stroked my hair. "There,
there, baby," she said, "you just let it out. Lord knows we all
have reason enough to cry."

That was how Jake and the others found us: crying in each
other's arms.

They stood there in the doorway to the kitchen, covered in
mud from head to foot and with grass stains on their jeans. I
was amazed at how much Brian looked liked Pa: dark hair,
bushy brows and sturdy as a concrete wall. John favored Jake
in looks, with his sand-blond hair and slighter frame. Still, I
thought, *neither of them is as handsome as my Jake.*

John's brow wrinkled in concern when he saw the tears on
our faces. Brian dropped his gaze to the floor, and Jake looked

like he wanted to crawl back in whatever hole they'd just come out of. He stood there sweating, holding out a rusty, five-pound can that had once held pork and beans.

"It's empty," he said, setting the can on the table. "Someone beat us to it."

No one else said anything. We all knew in our hearts who that someone was, but no one wanted to say it in front of Ma.

"I know what you're all thinkin'," Ma said, "and maybe you're right. Maybe our Davy did take the money. But it's no never mind. You all got good jobs and been making it on your own awhile now. I've got social security; I'm not going to starve. It seems like the only one of us who really needed cash has it now. I say God bless him, and let it go." She glared at her three sons, as if daring them to contradict her.

None of them did. Brian mumbled, "I've got to get to work," kissed his mother's cheek and headed out the door. John kissed her too and followed on his brother's heels.

Jake went over to the sink and washed his face and hands. Then he stood behind me and gave my shoulders a gentle squeeze. "I'll come back tomorrow and board up the well again," he said, like we'd just been there for a Sunday visit. "The cover's no good for anything but kindling."

C h a p t e r
T e n

May settled softly into June. Santa Ana winds scoured the sky to a brilliant blue, erasing the noxious veil of smog. Then the air calmed, and a summer sprinkle dampened the dusty ground. The hummingbirds took full advantage. They ignored the feeder and dipped their beaks into dew-washed fuchsias and the riot-colored sweet peas climbing the patio wall.

Libby seemed to have forgotten all about Miguel. She finished out her junior year with the usual A's and B's and took a summer job tending four children for a friend of Dotty's.

"Are you sure you can handle it, honey?" I asked when she told me she'd be working from ten o'clock in the morning to six at night, and fixing lunch and dinner besides.

"Mother! I'll be fine. Mrs. Mathers says the baby sleeps all day and the older ones play with their friends. It'll be a cinch. Besides, Rachel said she'd help me when she's not at one of Freddy's ball games." Freddy was Rachel's latest boyfriend. He had graduated in June and landed a spot on a summer hardball league. Jake was impressed when Sam told us about the boy.

"He must be good," he confided to me on the way home from an evening of pinochle at the Levis'. "They don't just take any rookie kid right out of high school. This is a triple-A team. Why can't Libby find a boy like that?"

"Jake, hush!" I instinctively looked into the back seat, but Libby had stayed late at the Matherses' so the parents could go to a show. "Libby will be just fine, darling," I promised. "She'll find a nice young man and settle down someday. Then we'll look back on these years and laugh."

Jake didn't look convinced, but for a change he didn't dwell on the subject. As soon as we walked in the door, he began digging into boxes in the hall closet. Ten minutes later he emerged from a pile of old books, shoe skates and galoshes with the fielder's glove he'd used in high school.

"Good as new!" He beamed. From somewhere he unearthed a can of leather oil and sat up until midnight rubbing it into the old glove, whistling "Take Me Out to the Ball Game." He hadn't played baseball in years. But it was the first time I'd seen him truly content since his father died, so I took a book into the bedroom and let him be.

Libby came in around eleven. "Boy, Dad's sure in a good mood."

I nodded. "I think he wants to play baseball again."

She rolled her eyes. "I didn't think men his age could still run the bases." She gave me the same Cheshire-cat grin Jake used to tease me with, and backed toward the door. "I'm going to bed. See you in the morning."

Just before I drifted into sleep, I thought how surprised I was that Libby was doing so well with all those kids.

* * *

Uncle Edward seldom talked on the phone. "I like to look people in the eye when I talk to them," he always said. "That way I don't just hear their words, I can see what they really mean." So when he phoned right after breakfast on Saturday morning and talked for twenty minutes straight, I thought something bad had happened and he was afraid to tell me.

Chapter Ten

"No, no." He apologized when I interrupted the flow of words
to ask if anything was wrong. "It's just . . . well, Rose hasn't
been herself lately, and I thought maybe a visit from you would
lift her spirits. I'm sure she's looking for a good excuse to cook
a big Sunday dinner." He paused, and I was appalled at how
desperate he sounded.

"Of course we'll come," I assured him. "Tell Aunt Rose I'll
bring a potato salad."

After I hung up, I remembered we were scheduled to have
dinner tomorrow with Dotty and Sam. "I don't have the heart
to call back and tell him no," I told Jake. "I'm sure Dot will
understand."

Dot insisted we go to San Bernardino, of course. "You see us
all the time," she said. "Zeke will be disappointed; he wanted to
play catch with Jake. But I'll talk Sam into buying him some
new baseball cards. That will cheer him up."

I tried to stave off my guilty conscience by being mad at
Mary Margaret. After all, she was Uncle Edward and Aunt
Rose's daughter. Why didn't she visit them more often? But the
truth was, we'd been so involved with Libby and Jake's family
lately that we'd neglected Aunt Rose and Uncle Edward ourselves.

I put some eggs on to boil and dug out a pan for the potatoes.
To my dismay, there were only two small ones left in the drawer.

"Oh, I forgot to tell you," Libby said as she grabbed an apple
from the basket on the table. "The kids got a Mr. Potato Head
game. Mrs. Mathers was out of potatoes, if you can imagine, so
I took some over."

Before I could scold her, a horn honked in the driveway.
"There's Carol," Libby mumbled and swallowed a mouthful of
fruit. "We're going to the library. Bye." She grabbed another
apple and bolted out the door.

The eggs were boiling over, and the water in the other pot had started to steam. I snatched the egg pan off the stove and mopped up the mess with a dishrag.

"Whew, what's that smell?" Jake came from the living room rubbing a baseball into the pocket of his softened leather glove. He eyed the pan of eggs and the piles of fresh-cut pickles and onions. "Hey, potato salad! Save some out for us, okay?" He slapped my arm, then bolted for the living room. "Rats! Roger Maris just hit another homer and I missed it."

I closed my eyes, said a prayer for patience and dragged a bag of elbow macaroni off the shelf. Macaroni salad would have to do.

* * *

Libby went along to Aunt Rose's without a fuss, and, to my relief, Mary Margaret wasn't there.

"She's testing for her CPA certificate this weekend," Uncle Edward fairly crowed. "It's a tough exam, but she can handle it."

"I hope so." Aunt Rose set a dish of candy on the coffee table. "Move your feet, Edward; they belong on the floor." She turned to me and went on without a pause. "Mary Margaret didn't get much sleep this week, and I know she's not eating right.

"Libby Jane, be a good girl and help me set the table."

The ham and baked beans were delicious, as usual, and no one complained about the macaroni salad. Given Aunt Rose's unusual behavior, I think Jake was afraid she would send him to his room if he said anything. We switched the conversation away from Mary Margaret, but nothing we talked about seemed to stop Aunt Rose from fretting. "I can't understand why our Chuck won't stop hedging and let God have his way with him. He and Anne Marie belong together," she said. "Libby, you look peaked, sweetheart. I'm afraid those little ones are too much for you. You're not seventeen yet yourself."

On the way home Libby asked, "Man, what's wrong with Nana Rose? She was sure bossy today."

"I'm sure she's fine, hon," I tried to convince us both. "Maybe she's overtired."

Libby shrugged and went back to staring out the window, a dreamy smile on her face. *Aunt Rose's behavior couldn't have bothered her too much.* But it bothered me.

"I can't imagine what's gotten into Aunt Rose," I told Jake that night after Libby had gone to her room. "She seems so out of sorts. It's not like her at all."

Jake chuckled. "I know. I've never heard Edward say a bad word about Rose, but he told me today she's driving him crazy. I guess she's been treating him like a two-year-old, fussing over everything and nothing for months now."

"I wonder if I should insist she see a doctor."

Jake shook his head. "Edward already did that. She admitted she had been feeling tired lately, so she went in for a checkup. Edward says everything's fine. The doctor told her to relax more—read a book or watch TV." Jake laughed. "I guess she told him her private life was none of his concern." He yawned and began unbuttoning his shirt. "If you ask me, she's probably just bored. Edward ought to build her a greenhouse or buy her a dog."

"A dog? Jake Freeman, the last thing Aunt Rose needs is a dog to clean up after."

"Now don't you start," Jake warned as he slipped into his pajama top. "One pushy woman in the family is enough." He pulled back the covers, stretched out on the bed and patted the sheet beside him.

"You should have seen his face when I picked up my book and said I was going to read for an hour," I told Dotty later. "I might as well have told him I was flying to the moon. He still hasn't figured out what made me mad, and if he doesn't know, I'm not going to tell him."

Chapter
Eleven

The Fourth of July always brings special memories. And not just because of Libby's birthday. She turned seventeen July 4, 1961, but I had almost forty years of celebrations to remember. Most of them were grand events with noisy parades, ball games in the park and flashy fireworks lighting up the nighttime sky.

I had baked Libby's favorite chocolate cake the night before, but got up at dawn to finish up the beans and fry the chicken. The early-morning quiet soothed my spirit. I was free to daydream and talk to God—things I used to do in the evening on the back porch steps. But those quiet times had been few and far between lately. I hadn't really thought about how much I missed them until that day.

I pictured Mama in her chair by Krista's crib, the big black Bible open on her lap, her lips forming silent words. "It's called prayer, Cissy," she told me one day when I was five. "I'm talking to God."

"Like we do in church?" I asked.

I'll never forget the sparkle in her eye. "Yes, Cissy, but you don't have to be in church to talk to God. He hears you anytime, anywhere you are." She laid the Bible aside and pulled me onto her lap. "Remember that, sweet girl, and you won't ever feel alone." I could feel her gentle hands caress my hair, and the softness of her pink chenille robe. She smelled like laundry soap and lavender cologne.

A spit of grease landing on my arm made me realize a tear had dropped into the frying pan. I wiped my eyes with the edge of a napkin and quickly moved the chicken pieces to a paper towel. *Get it together, girl,* I told myself. *It's supposed to be a happy day.*

By nine o'clock Jake had loaded everything but the cooler into the Chevy, and Carol was knocking on the door.

"Hi, Mrs. F., is Libby ready? I want to get a spot right on the shore." She dumped her beach towel and suntan lotion into Jake's recliner and hurried into Libby's room. "You're not really wearing that old thing!" I heard her squeal before she slammed the door.

"Carol's really a very sweet girl," I'd told Aunt Rose the other day. "A little too boy-crazy, but she's a year older than Libby and I suppose that's to be expected."

We all wanted to get an early start. Huntington Beach was crowded during the summer, even more so on the Fourth, but it was Libby's favorite place to celebrate, and we'd stayed home the last three birthdays in a row.

We met Dot and Sam in Lot C by ten o'clock, as planned, but the beach was already crowded with sunbathers. We wove our way through a group of children tossing a bright inflated ball and found an open area about halfway to the water. Libby, Carol and Rachel made their way closer to the waves and managed to squeeze all three towels into a sunny spot right next to the lifeguard station. David started to follow, then thought better of it and spread his towel on a strip of sand several yards away.

Jake and Sam raced the younger children to the water. Dot and I read awhile, then spread out the picnic lunch. The older girls were coaxed back to our blankets by the smell of food and the pile of brightly colored packages I had laid out on the sand.

Libby oohed and aahed over an aqua scarf from Rachel and the new Beach Boys record Carol gave her. Her gift from Dotty and Sam was a stunning black-and-white spaghetti-strap dress from Robinson's. I thought Libby was going to faint when she opened it. She held it up to whistles and whoops from David and the girls, but when some young men throwing a football a few yards away joined in, she blushed and folded it carefully back into the box.

"Thank you, Aunt Dotty." Libby reached over and wrapped her in a hug. "It's the most beautiful thing I've ever owned."

I was glad she couldn't see her father's face.

I smiled when Jake looked up at me and motioned to the bag at his feet. He nodded, drew out the birthday card we'd signed, and slid it over Libby's shoulder. "Here, sweetheart, this is from your mother and me. Happy birthday."

Libby looked puzzled as she opened the envelope, then gasped and sprang to her feet. "Oh, Daddy. Thank you, thank you. I can't believe it!"

I thought Carol and Rachel were going to burst. "What is it? Let us see!" Carol grabbed for the card, and the other blue and white envelope fluttered to the ground. Rachel pounced on it, and the three of them managed to act like four-year-olds at a circus.

"They're tickets!" Carol screamed.

Rachel spun the envelope out of Carol's reach and gasped. "Airplane tickets. To San Francisco!"

"San Francisco? Oh, you lucky duck! My folks would never let me go to San Francisco by myself."

"I won't be by myself." Libby retrieved the ticket and smiled at me from behind her friend's ponytail. "I'm going to visit my Aunt Anne. For three whole weeks."

Chapter Eleven

The sparklers we lit for the younger ones that night couldn't begin to match the light in Libby's eyes. She adored her Aunt Anne and my brother Chuck. She'd been pestering us to take her for a visit, but Jake didn't want to leave the shop. "Besides," he'd said when I brought it up, "when you and I go on vacation, it will be somewhere more exotic than San Francisco."

It had only been a few weeks ago that he'd surprised me by coming home for lunch on a Tuesday afternoon. I'd been cleaning out the refrigerator, trying to decide what to fix for dinner, when he popped through the kitchen door.

"Jake Freeman, what are you doing home? It's the middle of the day."

He looked at his watch and clutched his chest in mock horror. "Egad, woman, you're right, and I'm hungry as a wolf." He eyed the food spread out all over the table and grinned. "I don't think I can eat all this, though." He moved the empty ice-cube trays to the sink and pulled up a chair. "Fix me a sandwich, and I'll show you Libby's birthday present."

"Libby's present? What on earth . . . I hadn't even thought about it."

He looked smug. "Well, I have. I called Anne Marie, and she said she'd be glad to have Libby come for a few weeks. She won't be able to get the whole time off, but they can visit. Between her and Chuck, Libby will get a grand tour of San Francisco."

"Oh, darling, she'll be thrilled! But won't that be expensive?"

His grin faded to a rueful smile. "Yes, but it's what Libby really wants. Besides, if she's in San Francisco with Anne, she won't be running loose all summer."

He didn't say she'd be far away from Miguel, but he was thinking it; I could see it in his eyes.

* * *

Libby was to leave the second week in August, but when a

man with a gun took over an airplane and forced the pilot to fly him to Cuba, we almost didn't let her go.

"She can't go alone now," I told Jake after we saw the news reports on TV. "That man could have shot up the entire plane. And what on earth would she do if she wound up in Cuba?"

But a spokesman from the airlines insisted it was just a fluke. "We've increased security and are taking all the necessary precautions," he told the reporter for channel 4. "The public can rest assured that nothing like this will ever happen again."

* * *

I was surprised at how fast the summer flew with Libby gone. I'd expected to be bored to tears with the housework caught up and no one but Jake and myself to do for. But I managed to fill my time with visits to Aunt Rose and helping Ma Freeman fix up her house.

"A little paint and maybe some wallpaper in the bathroom will do wonders," I told her.

Every time I went over there, I grew more and more angry with Dave. As the months went by and he didn't put in an appearance, we were even more convinced he'd stolen the money from the well. If there had been any, that is.

"The can was old," Brian had offered in Dave's defense, "almost rusted through. Maybe the money disappeared a long time ago."

Of course we couldn't know for sure that Dave had taken it. But he had stolen cash from Jake's till, so that proved he was a thief. Besides, like I told Dotty, "Anyone who would leave his widowed mother alone and almost penniless, when he could very well be working to help support her, is capable of anything."

Jake refused to discuss his brother Dave, or anything else he considered unpleasant. He came home more often for lunch and sometimes, on weekends, suggested picnics in the park. "I like having you to myself," he said one day. "Not that I won't be glad to see Libby again. But it's nice to have some time alone."

Chapter
Twelve

Libby came home at the end of August. We picked her up at the airport and sighed with relief when we saw her coming off the plane. There'd been no more skyjacking, but I had to admit I'd been nervous about her flight back home.

She talked nonstop on the hour drive from L.A. to San Gabriel. "We rode the cable cars and drove across the Golden Gate Bridge. Chinatown was a blast. And, oh man, the food! We had lobster at Fisherman's Wharf and hot-fudge sundaes at Ghirardelli Square. I must have gained ten pounds." She smoothed the fabric of her new slacks over a nonexistent tummy bulge.

"Uncle Chuck made me chicken cordon bleu at *his* restaurant and taught me to drive. He has the coolest candy-apple-red Corvette. I can park on hills and everything!"

I thought Jake was going to park right there in the left-hand lane of the San Bernardino Freeway. "Chuck taught you how to drive in a Corvette?" His tone was even, but his knuckles on the steering wheel were turning white.

Libby must have heard the steel in his voice, because her own tone dropped an octave or two. "It's no big deal, Dad. Chuck says I'm almost as good a driver as him."

I gave Jake a warning look. We had both agreed that when

Libby came home we'd do our best to keep peace. She had experienced her first taste of freedom and had had time to forget about Miguel. "Libby will be on her own in a year or so," I'd reminded Jake just the day before. "We should enjoy her while we can."

"Why don't we stop for lunch at Toni's?" I suggested now. "Doesn't a pizza sound good?"

Jake's mouth snapped shut, and he pulled into the right-hand lane to catch the Rosemead Boulevard exit. To my relief, Libby went on to sing the praises of the little pizza place Anne Marie had taken her to, then launched into an enthusiastic description of some of the meals Chuck had prepared.

When my brother had finished his parole time for the stolen motorcycle and followed Anne Marie to San Francisco, the only job experience he'd had was "slinging hash" in a few small-time cafés. To everyone's surprise, he landed a job as an assistant chef in a family restaurant and decided to pursue cooking as a career. Now, five years later, he was the head chef at Arturo's, one of the nicest dinner houses on the wharf. By all accounts, he was doing well. Financially, at least.

Libby confided later that he had attended church with her and Anne Marie. "He sang the songs and everything. But when Anne asked if he enjoyed the sermon, he just shrugged and looked at the ground." She sighed. "Sundays were a drag. We went out to dinner after church, but no one talked much and neither of them smiled. By Monday they were all lovey-dovey again." She stared out the window, a dreamy smile on her face. "They belong together, Mom. I don't understand why they don't just get married."

"It's not always that easy," I hedged, and was relieved when Libby dropped the subject.

* * *

I had planned on taking Libby school shopping the last week

in August, but Anne Marie had helped her put together quite a wardrobe; the only thing she needed was new shoes. We found a pair of plain black flats that would work with skirts and dresses, and decided her sneakers would last a few more months.

Libby spent the next few days catching up with Rachel and Carol. All three girls badgered me to take Libby up to get her driver's license. "She's really a great driver, Mrs. F.," Carol insisted. "Better than me."

Rachel backed her up. "That's true, Aunt Celia. And just think how much time you'll save when Libby can drive herself places."

"Give me a chance, Mom. Most kids my age already have their license."

After several days of listening to their prattle, I gave in. She took the test in my Chevrolet and came back into the waiting room grinning like she'd just won the Indy 500. "I got a ninety-eight on the written exam," she bragged to Rachel, "and a ninety-five on the driving. The guy said I'll be fine as long as I don't have to parallel park."

I was glad to see her so happy. And Jake seemed to be feeling better too, now that things had picked up at the shop.

"We haven't been this busy since this time last year," he chuckled, and threw his greasy overalls into the laundry tub. "I had to help out in the pits today."

I smiled at his enthusiasm. He would rub his hands together and mumble about the vacation fund, but I knew that money wasn't his main concern. He was proud of the reputation his shop had earned in the community, and rightfully so. He was honest and fair, and the two mechanics he'd hired were good at their jobs.

* * *

On September 2 my sister Florence called to wish me happy

birthday. She and Jerry had already sent a card, but she wanted to say how she'd missed seeing me this summer and find out when we could have lunch again. We made a lunch date for a week from Tuesday.

"I'm sure Stuart will want to come," Florence said. "We had him out to dinner last week, and he said he misses our little get-togethers too."

I felt a flush of excitement. "It'll be good to get back to my old routine," I told Dotty. "I'm going to talk Jake into letting me find another job. I miss working as much as I miss my lunches with Flo." *And Stuart,* I admitted.

* * *

"Well, you look pretty chipper tonight for someone just a year away from forty." Jake grinned and kissed me on the cheek. "And all dressed up too," he teased. "Are you going somewhere?"

"I'd better be, Jake Freeman. You promised me steak and shrimp at the Silver Swan." I tugged his chin and kissed him on the lips, knowing full well I'd leave a blot of lipstick there. "Besides"—I slid away before he could retaliate—"Dotty says she only has lobster once a year, on my birthday, and this afternoon she was almost drooling just talking about it."

Jake's eyes danced. "Well, okay, I guess I'd better cancel our reservations at the Mighty Dog and hop in the shower. I wouldn't want to make Dotty mad; she might ground me for a week."

We rang the Levis' bell at seven, and I was immediately engulfed in hugs and kisses. Mikey grinned and handed me a homemade card. He'd drawn a stick lady with scarecrow hair and a butcher knife the size of a meat cleaver. She was bending over a birthday cake that sported one large candle. "It's a firecracker," he explained proudly. "Thirty-nine candles is too many to draw."

Libby and Rachel had already driven away in my car to baby-sit the Mathers kids. Rachel had taken over Libby's job when she went to San Francisco, but it had only lasted a week.

"I don't know how Libby did it," Dotty had confided after Rachel came home in tears for the third night in a row. "Those children are a handful. If you ask me, that woman should stay home and raise them herself."

Mrs. Mathers had wound up hiring someone from an agency, and Rachel agreed to baby-sit at night when they were all ready for bed. Libby decided to help her tonight, which left David to stay home with his siblings.

"School starts in just a few days," Dotty reasoned as she decreed an eight-o'clock bedtime. "You need to get used to going to bed early again." Before their protests could turn into a riot, she kissed them all goodby and ruffled David's hair.

"You guys be good and mind your brother," Sam interjected, "or no television for a week."

* * *

Dinner was wonderful. I had just declared myself too full to eat another bite, when Jake suggested we go into Hollywood for a movie and have dessert at the Metropolitan.

"Whoa, when did you get to be Daddy Warbucks?" Sam grinned and put his share of a substantial tip on the table.

Jake studied the tab again and whistled. "Maybe you're right. I guess we'd better make that ice cream at the Foster's Freeze."

Dotty groaned. "I don't think I can handle the thought of a chocolate dip on top of lobster. Anyway"—she looked at Sam—"we should get home. There's no telling what that crew is up to."

Sam nodded. "I'm afraid Dot's right. David has a habit of hiding behind a book and forgetting the rest of the world. That could be a disaster with the twins and Mikey.

"Happy birthday, doll." Sam kissed me on the cheek. "And try not to get any older, will ya? We have to age right along with you."

We said good night at the curb. Jake didn't turn on the radio like he usually did. Instead he patted the seat next to him and drove home with his arm around my shoulders.

He pulled into the driveway and tugged me toward him for a kiss. "Well, babe, are you ready for your real gift?" His voice was husky, and his eyes gleamed like the candle on our dinner table.

"Jake," I whispered, "we're too old for this. What will the neighbors think?"

He chuckled and pressed a finger to my lips. "Do you really care what the neighbors think?"

An owl-eye moon peeked between the branches of the maple tree. We had rolled the windows down, and I could feel the feather-light breeze as it flicked leafy shadows across the driveway, splashing our faces with flecks of light. It reminded me of the night Jake had proposed—the two of us huddled together in the front seat of Uncle Edward's car.

"Celia?"

I blinked and realized Jake was holding something out to me. It was an envelope similar to the one we had given Libby. Sure enough, when I opened the card, a blue and white packet fluttered into my lap.

"What on earth?" I held the tickets up to the light, but Jake couldn't wait for me to decipher the small type.

"Hawaii, babe, just the two of us. I promised you fun in the sun, remember?"

Then it dawned on me: the vacation fund had finally paid off.

Chapter
Thirteen

Before I had a chance to call Aunt Rose, Jake's mother asked to keep Libby while we were away. "Please let her stay here," Ma begged. "She'll be such company for me. I do miss the young ones around the house." I couldn't imagine how she could miss Dave and his shenanigans, but I knew she did. And the others led such scattered, busy lives. Jake and I were the only ones she saw on a regular basis. Brian and John lived nearby, but Brian was engaged and John was married to his career. I knew they loved their mother, but their idea of showing it was to let her cook them dinner once a month.

"I have to go, Mom," Libby said solemnly. "Grandma Freeman needs me."

Jake and I agreed without too much hesitation. As far as we knew, Dave was still in Mexico—and not likely to show his face around home for a while. Aunt Rose was lonely too, but she had Uncle Edward and we knew she'd understand.

"How nice for Ella," Aunt Rose said when I explained that Libby would stay with her grandmother. "It will be a blessing for her to have Libby around."

With that detail out of the way, I spent the months of October and November hunting for a bathing suit and making clothes.

"Mom, that's so square!" Libby shouted when she saw the pretty, flower-print skirted swimsuit I had found on sale at Penny's. "You need a two-piece and sundresses and shorts, not all these cotton slacks and blouses. Honestly! You'd think you were a grandmother or something."

"What do you think?" I asked Florence the next day. We were shopping at La Cher, a little boutique a few blocks from campus. Neither Jerry nor Stuart had been able to get away for lunch, and I had given up asking Jake, so we were on our own. Flo had suggested we might "just look at a few things" and maybe get some ideas.

"I think Libby is right," she said. "You still have a pretty good figure. Why resort to old-lady clothes if you don't have to?" She held up two strips of flimsy blue nylon attached to a tiny drawstring bag. "Look, this one's perfect, and it comes with its own carry bag."

She must have seen the look of horror on my face. "Okay, okay, we'll compromise." She grinned and led me to a rack of suits in sizes 5 through 9.

To my surprise, I found I could still wear a size 7, and we decided on a low-cut, backless rib-knit in a baby blue. It was a one-piece, but later even Libby agreed it suited me.

"Wow, that's boss. You'll knock Dad's socks off!"

Secretly, I hoped she was right.

* * *

December was cooler than usual that year. We'd been bundled in sweaters since Thanksgiving, and by Dave and Amy's birthday on the fifth, I had to dig out my old wool coat.

Ma Freeman had insisted on cooking dinner, as usual. I brought the cake, just like I did every year, but this time, instead of writing "Happy Birthday, Dave and Amy" on it, I decorated it with icing flowers and tiny bright balloons.

"Just think, they're twenty-four now, babe," Jake said. "Amy isn't going to care if her name's not on the cake." He turned his head, but I caught the look of sadness on his face. "At least it'll be a relief not to have to put up with Dave's attitude."

I knew there'd be no shortage of heavy hearts that day. Their pa had been a little rough around the edges, but they missed him terribly. If the truth were told, they all missed Davy too.

Libby sulked most of the afternoon, and I wondered if she had secretly hoped her Uncle Dave would show up for the party.

* * *

Jake and I agreed that we wouldn't buy Christmas presents for each other that year. "The trip will be enough for several Christmases and birthdays put together," I vowed.

"Right," Jake grinned. "Don't worry, babe. I'm not dumb enough to try and hold you to that."

I still had to shop for Libby and the others, though. Jake's family was becoming so large, we'd agreed to draw names. I'd drawn Brian's name and had no idea what to get him. Jake was no help at all. "I don't know," he said when I asked for some suggestions. "Get him a tie or socks or something. That's your department, woman."

It was Stuart who saved the day. I had seen him only twice that entire autumn. The day after my birthday in September, when he handed me a friendship card and a single rose, and the afternoon I'd picked up Florence for our shopping trip at La Cherí. He'd been up to his neck in paperwork that day, muttering something about how he needed an assistant and if the school wouldn't provide one he'd just have to see to it himself.

Then Flo and Jerry invited us to a Christmas party at their house in mid-December. Jake and Jerry huddled in the corner most of the evening, drinking cherry soda and talking football. I thought Stuart was involved in their conversation, but when I complained to Flo that I still couldn't think of anything for

Brian, he spoke up.

"How about a book, Celia? What does he like to read?"

"I don't know. He's not much of a scholar, but I'm sure he must like to read."

"Something light, then. A western maybe? I like Louis L'Amour myself."

I bought L'Amour's latest book the next day. Jake and I laughed when we read the excerpt on the back cover. "All I wanted was enough to buy a ranch," it read, "but gold has a way of its own with men."

When Brian opened his gift on Christmas Eve, his face lit up with pleasure. "Hey, thanks, I've been wanting this book."

"Who would have guessed?" I said to Jake that night. "I'll have to thank Stuart for suggesting it."

Jake just scowled and turned out the light.

*　*　*

We dropped Libby off at six o'clock the morning after Christmas and made our eight a.m. flight to Honolulu.

It was my second trip to Hawaii. In 1943 I had flown to Oahu for a short visit with Jake during the war. I shed bitter tears when I learned he was shipping out again. As it turned out, Libby was conceived that same night, and so my memories of the island were sweet. We had taken the same flight path then as now, but during the war I hadn't been able to see Waikiki or Diamond Head from the air. This time I gaped in wonder at the dazzling strip of shell-white sand and the stark gray rock jutting out to sea.

Jake pointed down to a huge enclosure guarded by a ring of vegetation and coconut palms. I knew without his saying it that it was the Navy base where he'd been stationed so many years ago.

We stepped off the plane into another world. The sun-warm air hung heavy with the smell of jasmine and ginger. Clusters of half-ripe fruit clung to coconut palms and banana trees, their leaves rustling like wind chimes in a summer breeze. Winter never laid an icy palm against these islands, although, as Jake reminded me later, tropical storms and volcanoes caused as much destruction as any mainland snow.

Our cabby, a young Hawaiian dressed in bright-green shorts and a loud yellow shirt, pointed out the sights. "You want jewelry or baskets, the Market Place has everything you need. Better prices than the stores in town. Waikiki is just a mile up ahead. On your right's the Royal Hawaiian. They used it as a hospital during the war."

Jake winced, then pasted a smile on his face and handed the driver a generous tip when he dropped us at the door of our hotel.

Honolulu's two main streets were lined with restaurants and hotels. There were bars and shops and grocery stores, but these were small, and they blended so well into the landscape that I hardly even noticed.

"Wait until you see the other side of the island," Jake promised, as he led me past the crowded Market Place and down a short flight of stairs to the restaurant we had chosen for dinner. "We'll go over to the north shore tomorrow, and you can see what the real Hawaii looks like."

Chapter
Fourteen

Elephant ears and banyan trees, a monster surf swallowing the shore. We walked slowly, savoring the lush, damp beauty, struggling to breathe in the heavy air. A small green lizard skittered across the path. "Those are geckos," Jake had told me the night before. "They're harmless, and they keep the bugs at bay." After that, I found I hardly noticed them.

I noticed the spiders, though. There were hundreds of them on the island, most concealed in the heavy foliage, but the one I dreaded was the banana spider, a huge tarantulalike beast with visible fangs. One had crawled across the living room of our suite, and I'd refused to get out of bed that morning until Jake checked over the entire floor.

It was our fifth day on the island. My skin was the color of a ripe pomegranate from days of basking on Waikiki Beach and swimming in the sun-warmed ocean. "One more day, babe." Jake smiled and took my hand. "There's a New Year's Eve bash at the hotel tomorrow night, then we're off to Maui. Are you having fun?"

"Oh, Jake," I sighed, "you know I am. I don't even want to think about going home. Not that I don't miss Libby," I added quickly, "and the rest of our family. Wouldn't it be nice to bring them here? Aunt Rose and your mother would love it."

Jake laughed, and I had to admire the way his teeth sparkled white against his dark-tanned face. He was more relaxed than I'd seen him in years.

"Now that would be romantic! Rose would want to dust and vacuum and make the beds before the maid came in, and Ma would fret about the price of meals. She'd have me out fishing for our dinner in two days' time."

I laughed with him and swung his hand as we walked back to the rental car. "Let's take one more moonlight sail before we leave."

"It will have to be tonight. I have to run an errand in the morning, and we'll want to rest up for tomorrow night." His tone was casual, but he avoided my eyes as he opened the passenger door and slipped around to the driver's side.

"What kind of errand would you have to run here?"

"Pearl Harbor. The new memorial. It's just something I have to do."

I shuddered. The Arizona Memorial. I remembered a few months back when President Kennedy approved a bill to fund construction. They called it "the final resting place for 1,100 Navy men and Marines who lost their lives defending the U.S.S. *Arizona.*" I thought about the other ships that had been stationed there on Battleship Row: the *Oklahoma* and the *California,* the *Ohio, Utah, Maryland, Pennsylvania,* and the *Tennessee.* And the *West Virginia,* where so many of Jake's buddies had died and my husband nearly lost his life. The memorial was to be a tribute to them as well, a reminder of the cost of war in human lives.

I laid my hand on his thigh. "Are you sure you want to do that, Jake? I didn't even think it was open yet."

He cradled my hand with his own and caressed my knuckles with his thumb. "I don't *want* to go—I have to. I don't expect you to understand." He looked at me, but it was obvious his

thoughts were far away. "I have connections," he said, and I
knew it was best to let the matter drop.

* * *

Jake stayed quiet all through breakfast. We sipped coffee and
watched as men and women with sun-browned bodies swung
down the boulevard, beach bags balanced on their hips and
straw mats tucked beneath their arms. They chattered gaily,
shielding their eyes against morning glare, hurrying to find a
basking place on the narrow strip of sand.

I had worn a yellow sundress with a short white linen jacket
and low-heeled sandals. If Jake was so determined to resurrect
old ghosts, I wasn't going to let him do it alone. I'd lain awake
most of the night gathering my defenses; I expected him to
protest. But when the time came to leave, he simply opened the
car door and helped me in. He held on to the door frame and
bent his head toward mine. "Can you handle this, Celia?" When
I nodded yes, he straightened up and shut the door.

We headed west out of Honolulu on the Kamehameha High-
way. Twenty minutes later we passed a sign that said "Pearl
Harbor Naval Base" and parked beside a guard post. Jake got
out and approached a young man in dress whites. Jake handed
him some papers, they spoke for a minute or two, then the
young man turned back into the hut that served as a guard
station and picked up a phone.

Ten minutes later we shook hands with an impressive gray-
haired commander who acted like he'd known Jake all his life.
"Jake Freeman. If I remember right, you were a cocky young
son-of-a-gun. Had the world by the tail, as I recall."

Jake grinned and shook his head. "Not me, sir, that was my
buddy Roy. I was the quiet one with the girl back home." He
motioned in my direction.

The commander's attention immediately shifted to me. "Ah,
and I see you kept her. You lucky dog." He clasped my hands

gently in both of his. "How have you put up with this son-of-a-monkey's-uncle all these years?"

Not waiting for a reply, he turned back to Jake. "*West Virginia,* was it? Well, we're not quite finished out there, but Lieutenant Dougan will do his best to show you around." He motioned to a young officer who had been waiting at attention beside the guard post. The officer hurried over and, after a smart salute for the commander, led us past the hut and across a parking lot to the harbor.

"We'll have to take the skiff," Lieutenant Dougan said, nodding apologetically toward a small white boat bobbing in the clean blue surf. "The officers' launch took off half an hour ago." Wishing I had chosen slacks and a blouse instead of a dress, I clung to Jake's hand as he helped me aboard, then settled as discreetly as I could on the bench seat beside him.

The lieutenant skillfully swung the boat around, and we chugged slowly toward the open bay. As we rounded the corner of a dock, he pointed straight ahead. "There it is. Impressive, don't you think?"

Impressive was too tame a word for the gleaming white concrete structure. "It's so long," I said.

Lieutenant Dougan nodded. "One hundred and eighty-four feet. It spans the entire ship."

The building bowed slightly in the middle. I counted seven observation windows, as well as seven skylights, and I knew the pattern would be repeated on the other side. As we drew closer, I could see the windows were empty of glass. Metal scraps and plastic-coated wire littered the dock area, and we picked our way carefully along the gangway and into the structure itself.

"Please watch your step," the lieutenant shouted over the sound of a worker's radio. "And try not to touch anything; the paint is wet." There wasn't much to see inside. Except for a few paint cans and the workman's ladder, the long, cavernous room was bare.

The lieutenant walked over to one of the observation windows and motioned toward the ocean. I had no idea what I was looking at, but at Jake's gasp, Lieutenant Dougan nodded. "Yes. It's the actual smokestack. We've left as much as possible undisturbed."

I looked closer and felt goosebumps crawl along my arms. The same incredibly clear blue sea that had allowed us to marvel at colorful angelfish, eels and playful dolphins now revealed the skeleton of a the battleship *Arizona.*

I swallowed my tears, certain that any show of emotion would undo Jake. He took my hand and gripped it hard. His face had paled beneath his tan, but his eyes were dry and not a muscle moved. It reminded me of a plaster cast of a famous composer I'd seen at the art museum.

How can he bear it? I thought. But the worst was yet to come.

I sometimes wonder what the rest of the trip would have been like if we had left right then. We might have taken just one more moonlight sail. We could have laughed and loved and enjoyed the last few blissful days of our vacation exploring the lush, green forests of Maui. But I don't dwell on that, because we didn't turn and go.

Lieutenant Dougan broke the silence. "The shrine chamber's not quite done. They're still doing some engraving, but you can get an idea of what it will look like." He led us through a door and into a small room where a wall of solid marble rose from floor to ceiling. There the names of the dead were etched in stone, a lasting commemoration of the gallant people who had given their lives for their country.

I watched as Jake scanned the unfinished list, looking for familiar names, perhaps trying to match them with less-familiar faces.

I watched and grieved and knew that nothing I could say would ease his pain.

Chapter
Fifteen

We went through the motions. Jake tried to deny his reawakened grief over the horror of Pearl Harbor and the fact that tomorrow was the anniversary of his father's death. I tried to pretend the vacation had not been ruined.

We called home that night from the phone in the hotel lobby to wish Ma and Libby happy new year. It was eleven p.m. in Los Angeles. Jake pressed his free hand over his ear to stifle the noise around us and waited for the connection. I was standing close so I could hear the conversation and say my own hellos. It took a couple of minutes to get through, but finally we heard the ringing and a click, then a male voice said dully, "Hello."

Jake stiffened and frowned. "Brian?"

"No, man. He ain't here. Who's this?"

"This is Jake . . ."

Another click, then the line went dead.

Jake slammed the receiver down and smacked the side of the phone box like he wanted to retrieve his coin. His face was as red as a fresh-cooked lobster, and I was glad it was too noisy to hear his muttered words.

"What on earth! Did we get a wrong number?"

"No, we did not get a wrong number. That was Dave. I'd bet my life on it." Jake took a deep breath, fished in his pocket for another coin and dialed again.

After what seemed like an eternity, Ma picked up the phone. "Hello, Jake?"

"Yes, Ma, it's me. What's going on over there?" He glanced at me, and I nodded to show I could hear.

"The children are having a party, for New Year's Eve. They can't mourn forever. Delbert would want them to have fun. Why are you calling? Is something wrong?"

"No, Ma, nothing's wrong," Jake lied, "we just wanted to make sure you were all right." He paused, and I thought he would ask to speak to Libby. Instead he cleared his throat and shouted over the noise, "Was that Dave who just picked up the phone?"

There was a pause on their end, and I thought we had lost the connection again. Then Ma's voice rattled through the static. "Yes, our Davy has come for a visit. Isn't that wonderful? We wanted it to be a surprise."

"Oh, it's a surprise, all right. Let me talk to him."

"Not now, dear. Sara June and the baby are here. Dave and Libby are showing them a new dance. Libby calls it the Twist. She wanted me to try, but I told her, 'Land, no. That would throw my back out for a month.' Libby's fine. Should I call her to the phone? Sara June can take her place."

"Yes!" I nodded hard and pulled on Jake's sleeve.

But he said, "No, if you're sure everything's okay, tell her we'll see her in a few days. And tell Dave to stick around. I want to talk to him when I get home."

"I will. Bye, my Jake. Give Celia my love, and have a happy time."

* * *

Maui: an island of tropical forests and dormant volcanoes,

waterfalls and deep, clear pools, pineapple groves and sugar-cane fields. We made the twenty-minute flight in half an hour against the wind. When we landed, a torrential rain began to fall. By the time we got our luggage into a taxi, we were soaked to the skin. The driver maneuvered his Volkswagen bus through ankle-deep water around the winding, pothole-filled road.

Our room in the hotel at Lahaina was small but clean and comfortable. By afternoon the rain had stopped. We explored the quaint little town with its wooden walkways and followed a trail of lava rock that flowed into the sea. Within an hour the sand was dry, but the ocean still responded to the sudden storm by throwing ten-foot waves against the shore.

"I've had enough sun for a while, anyway," I told Jake. "Let's have lunch and explore the island."

Jake shrugged and led me into a small café. We dined on fresh marlin, flat bread and homemade guava jelly. Jake paid for the meal and stifled a yawn. "Man, I could sure use a nap."

Suddenly I realized I was tired too. Neither of us had slept well the night before. If we were honest, we'd have to admit that the emotions of the past two days had caught up with us. I didn't say that to Jake, of course, but I did agree a restful afternoon sounded good. Jake slept for several hours, and I dug out a magazine.

The next morning, Jake hired a cab and we took a teeth-rattling ride to the inland village of Hana. To say the road was unpaved is like saying the ocean has some water in it; the road wound snakelike between wheel-bending boulders and cavern-ous potholes—on one side it hugged towering lava cliffs; on the other side it gave way to steep ravines that dropped perilously to the sea.

I held my breath at times, but was afraid that if I closed my eyes I would miss the collage of waterfalls, birds and tropical foliage that decorated the island. East of Lahaina, the crater Haleakala was rimmed in fog. Our driver and guide, a young man named Scott, pointed out several species of Hawaiian honeycreepers, slim-beaked birds of various colors and sizes, while we marveled at wild orchids, hibiscus and gardenias.

We stopped for lunch at Kipahulu, famous for its seven waterfalls that cascaded, stair-step fashion, into seven pools. It was a wild and wonderful place, and I thought for a while that we might find peace again.

While Scott sliced fresh pineapple and placed thick slabs of mahi-mahi on the grill, Jake and I wandered up and down the narrow trail beside the falls. Once we stopped to watch a mongoose feed, and Jake told me what he knew about the fascinating little creature.

"They were brought over to keep the rats under control. But rats are nocturnal and the mongoose hunts by day. So they survive on birds and fruit. Actually their favorite food is snake." He said it casually, but I could see a smile quirk at the corner of his mouth.

"Snakes?" I shuddered. I hadn't thought of snakes, but the heavy, junglelike undergrowth would be a haven for the slithery, creepy things. I stopped walking and grabbed Jake's arm.

It must have been the reaction he wanted. His smile grew until he laughed out loud, picked me up and held me over a philodendron bush big enough to swallow a full-grown man. I screamed and hung on for dear life. "Jake Freeman, don't you dare! Put me down right now!"

"Okay," he said agreeably, swinging me out even farther into the foliage.

I screamed again, and he turned back onto the trail just as Scott came panting to a stop beside us.

"Hey, don't do that, man!" Scott said. "You scared me to death."

I felt my face heat up, and Jake lowered me to the ground. "I was just going to show her the snakes."

Scott looked blank. "Snakes? There ain't no snakes on this island. Never have been." He looked at Jake, and a smile spread across his face. "You were telling her the mongoose story, right? Sorry, man, I thought something was really wrong. I mean, her screams sounded so real." His face grew more flushed with each apology. "I better go rescue lunch. Ten minutes, tops." He turned and hustled back down the trail.

My heart was still pounding, and I could barely breathe. "Jake Freeman, don't you ever do that again!" I smacked his arm for emphasis and tried to stay mad, but I had to admit it was good to see him smile.

Then his smile faded and his eyes grew sober. He took hold of my arms and fixed his eyes on mine. "I would never hurt you, Celia. You know that, don't you?" He pulled me up against his chest and put his cheek against my hair. "You're all I've got, Cissy girl. I could never bear to lose you. Never."

I hugged him tight and closed my eyes against his pain. "I'm here, darling. I'll always be here." *God willing.*

"Soup's on!" Scott's shout echoed up the trail.

Jake released me and led the way back to the car.

Chapter
Sixteen

When Libby was small, we would wake her for the first day back to school with a chorus of "School days, school days," a kiss on the cheek and her favorite breakfast. Now that she was a high-school senior, she was usually up before the rest of us, unwinding those hard pink plastic curlers from her hair and primping in the mirror. Once in a while, if she'd been up late the night before, she'd sleep till the last minute, then, in a state of panic, beg me to drive her so she wouldn't be late. Libby hated to be late for anything.

We'd been home three weeks, and except for our lingering tans, it was as if the vacation had never been. Jake was working longer hours than ever, while I had caught up on the house-work and had begun to make plans for a summer garden. The urge to find another job was growing stronger, but I knew Jake was opposed to it, and I didn't want to upset him just now.

He never brought up Pearl Harbor again, and I thought the new scratch on his emotions had probably healed. His father's death was still fresh for all of us, and I guessed that was why he was so angry with Dave for taking off again before they could "have a talk."

"Uncle Dave didn't take the money, Dad," Libby insisted.

"Grandma Freeman wouldn't bring it up, so I did, and Uncle Dave was really upset. He swore he didn't take it and said he'd—uh, get whoever did. I believe him and so does Grandma."

"Then why did he run like a scared rabbit?" Jake wasn't buying any of it. "Why didn't he stay and talk to me?"

"Because he knows you hate him, that's why!" There were real tears in Libby's eyes. "How can you hate your own brother? The Bible says that's a sin." She covered her mouth with both hands and fled to the bathroom.

Jake stared after her.

I tried to defuse the situation. "She didn't mean that, darling. You know she overreacts to everything."

Jake's shoulders drooped, and he waved my words away. "It's okay. She's wrong, but it's okay." He reached for his jacket on the coat rack by the door and slipped his arms into the sleeves. "I'm going out for a while. Don't wait supper for me."

He crawled into our bed at midnight. His skin was cool and smelled of exhaust smoke and fresh-cut grass. He was breathing fast, and I knew he'd been walking for hours.

The alarm went off at seven, and Jake got up as usual, but Libby didn't. I heard her in the bathroom about seven-thirty and couldn't help feeling irritated. I'd wanted to have my quiet time and make some phone calls this morning. Now I'd have to get dressed quickly and drive her to school.

Jake kissed me goodby. "See you tonight, babe. Have a good day."

"You too, darling." His cheerfulness, after last night, surprised me. *Maybe he really is okay,* I thought. If I could work my problems out in quiet, back-porch talks with God, why couldn't Jake deal with his on a nice long walk? I breathed a prayer of thanksgiving and knocked on Libby's door. At her answering groan, I pushed it open and found my daughter still in bed.

"Liberty Jane! I thought you were already up. You'll be late for school even if I drive you."

"I can't go, Mom. I've got the flu."

Her skin was pale and clammy. I rested my hand against her forehead, but she pushed it away and bolted out of bed toward the bathroom. When she returned, I stuck the thermometer in her mouth and fetched a cool cloth. The mercury registered 98.6. "No fever. But you're white as a sheet. Maybe it's just a twenty-four-hour bug." I kissed her cheek and handed her the cloth. "Keep this here, just in case. I'll go buy some soda crackers and some 7-Up."

She moaned again. "Thanks, Mom. All I want to do is sleep."

* * *

"We thought she was better," I told Dotty two weeks later. "She goes to school for a couple of days, then says she feels sick again."

"Maybe something's going on at school that's upsetting her. Have you talked to any of her teachers?"

"Are you kidding? Libby would rather die than have me call one of her teachers. Besides, she only has four classes this term and her grades are fine." I paused, grasping for straws. "I don't suppose Rachel or David has said anything?"

"No, but I can ask. Don't get your hopes up, though. David seldom notices anything beyond his books, and Rachel can be a clam where her friends are concerned. It would have to be really serious for her to say anything." Dotty went quiet for a minute. "You know, Celia, I hate to mention this, but the Clavely boy came down with mono last week. He's the third one at the high school since Christmas. Maybe you'd better have her checked."

Mononucleosis. Everyone called it "the kissing disease." I hadn't even thought of that, but it was possible. Libby dated some, but not as often as she had last year, and there was no one special that I knew of. Could she have been kissing Donald Clavely?

"Celia? I'm sorry, I didn't mean to scare you, but it is a possibility."

"No, I'm glad you told me. I was just thinking how awful it would be if she had to miss out on all the senior fun." I took a deep breath. "Well. No use howling before the milk is spilled. I'll make a doctor's appointment this afternoon."

Libby had a fit, of course.

"Mother, I don't need to go to the doctor," she insisted. "I'm perfectly fine—just tired, and my stomach feels sick once in a while. My gym teacher says it's probably just nerves, with graduation so close and all."

I hid my smile and kept my voice calm but firm. "Graduation is four months away. And you've never had a case of nerves in your entire life." I tried to sweeten the pill. "I'll tell you what. Your appointment is for three o'clock tomorrow. If you're feeling up to it afterward, we'll look for those white flats you've been pestering me to buy."

She looked less than mollified, but didn't argue further. Later, when I checked on her, she was curled up on top of the new flowered bedspread we had given her for Christmas, sound asleep. I covered her with an afghan and marveled at how much she had changed. It seemed that overnight my gangly, tangle-haired little girl had turned into a full-grown woman.

Her room smelled like Windsong, her favorite perfume. A pool of sunlight from the open window splashed across the pillow, highlighting shades of red in her light auburn hair. I studied the pale lashes that curved against her creamy cheeks, her flawless skin and the slender arms crossed over breasts that had grown more plentiful than mine.

She moaned and stirred, then clutched her chest tighter and settled back to sleep. Her face was toward me now—her pug nose and dainty chin, her naturally red lips pouting and full. She looked like Sleeping Beauty waiting for a kiss from her Prince Charming.

My heart thumped twice, then stilled and thumped again. I backed away, then stood stock-still in the middle of the room.

I knew.

As sure as night follows day, I knew. I wanted to scream or cry or run away, but I did nothing, just stood there breathing in the perfumed air as a dreadful stone-hard sadness claimed my soul.

"Oh, Mama," I finally whispered, "what are we going to do?"

Chapter
Seventeen

Grandma Eva used to say that trouble always comes in threes. If we counted Pa Freeman's passing and the situation with Jake's brother Dave, Libby's "illness" proved the theory out.

To my surprise, she gave up the fight and went to the doctor the following afternoon. "It's probably just a stubborn flu," he said as he ushered Libby back into the waiting room. "But we've taken some tests just to be sure nothing else is going on. We should have the results in a few days. In the meantime, maybe she should stay home from school. Just a precaution, of course. I'm sure her teachers would be glad to send her work home." He patted Libby's hand. "Get some rest, young lady. We'll have you right as rain in no time."

By the time we stopped for a Coke and picked up Libby's shoes, I had myself convinced the doctor was right. A few more days of rest and Libby would be back in school with the rest of her senior class, counting the days till graduation.

Libby, in fact, seemed to perk up that night. I fixed Swiss steak and lima beans for dinner. While she and Jake squabbled playfully over the last slice of bread, I served the ice cream I'd bought for dessert. Then Dotty called and blew Grandma Eva's theory to the moon.

* * *

"Something's wrong for sure," I told Jake on the way to Sam and Dotty's the following night. "We never get together on a weeknight. I hope no one is ill. But surely Dotty would have said? She wouldn't even hint at what was going on."

"Will you quit fretting, woman?" Jake's smile softened his words. "There's no sense jumping to conclusions; we'll find out soon enough."

It turned out to be too soon for me.

Dotty smiled when she let us in, but she hugged me hard and held onto Jake's arm just a fraction too long. "Come in and sit. I managed to hide a bag of chips from the kids, and Sam made onion dip."

"Speaking of kids," Jake chortled, "where are the little monkeys? I found an Indian-head nickel for David's coin collection and another baseball card for Zeke."

Dotty and Sam looked at each other like plotters of doom. "You can give the kids their trinkets later." Sam pointed Jake toward the sofa.

Dotty must have seen my alarm. "The kids are fine, Celia; they're all upstairs. We just wanted to talk to you guys alone."

Sam nodded. "There's no easy way to say this, so I'll just get it over with. Dotty and I are moving to Washington, D.C."

They could have pinned me to the carpet and I wouldn't have felt a thing. "Moving? When?"

"Why, you son-of-a-gun, you got the appointment!" Jake was on his feet shaking Sam's hand like he was pumping for water. "What a great career move! We'll miss you, of course, but to be on Robert Kennedy's staff! Way to go, buddy."

Sam was grinning ear to ear. "Finally, Jake. I finally get a chance to make a difference. Kennedy's big against organized crime. Those big-time hoods will find themselves face down in the mud before we're through."

Back in high school, some boys had talked Mary Margaret and me into sucking on some helium balloons. The gas made us dizzy and sick to our stomachs; when we tried to talk, the sounds we made sent us all into peals of laughter. My head and stomach felt like that now, but I never felt less like laughing in my life.

"Move? Dotty, you *can't* move. What about your home, and the children's school?" Jake just stared at me, and Dot looked like she was going to cry. *So what?* I thought. *She should cry. And so should Sam and Jake. What was the matter with them, acting like this was happy news?* To my dismay, I lowered my head and burst into tears.

Dotty ordered our astonished husbands upstairs to check on the children, then sat down and cried right along with me. We went through half a box of tissue before we blew our noses and Dotty explained about Sam's new job.

"He's wanted something like this for years, Celia. You know how he feels about fighting crime. It's what motivated him to become a lawyer in spite of—no, because of—his handicap. Sam sees this as a chance in a lifetime." She sighed and blew her nose again. "I don't want to move, girl, but my place is with Sam, it always has been. I can't deny him his dream."

I hugged her and said I understood. And I did, really, but that didn't make losing my best friends any easier. I swiped at a fresh tear and vowed not to make it harder on Dotty. "How are the kids taking it?"

She straightened her shoulders and forced a smile. "The younger ones are fine. David was alarmed at first. He's doing so well in school, he's afraid he might not be able to keep up somewhere else. But his physics teacher assured him he's smart enough to excel anywhere he goes. That seems to have reassured him.

"Rachel's a different story. We told the kids just two days

ago, and she stormed out in tears."

"Rachel? That doesn't sound like her."

Dotty nodded in agreement, "I know. We were shocked. Sam went in and had a talk with her, but she still can't understand why we have to leave. Now she won't talk to any of us. Sam feels really bad about it, but he says she'll come around. I'm surprised she didn't blab to Libby. We told her we'd appreciate it if we could break the news to you guys first, but she was so upset."

"I'm sure she never said a thing. Libby would have gone to pieces."

"Anyway," Dot continued, "I'll stay here with the kids until school's out and we sell the house. Sam can come home on weekends." She sighed again. "Life's a kick, isn't it, girl? The minute you think things are calm, it sucks you up and spits you into the storm."

"Amen," I heartily agreed.

* * *

We broke the news to Libby the next morning. She immediately burst into tears and fled to the bathroom, where she ran the water for a full twenty minutes before she reappeared, hollow-eyed and shaking.

"What's the matter with her lately?" Jake didn't try to hide his irritation. "She's always been emotional, but this is getting ridiculous."

"Maybe it's that time of the month for her," I said, even though I knew it probably wasn't so. "And anyway, Rachel is her best friend. How can you expect her to take their separation calmly?"

He rolled his eyes to the ceiling, like he wanted help from God, muttered something about "Women!" and headed for the car.

Libby forced herself to go to school, even though she still

loked weak and pale. My heart jumped when she came out of her room dressed in a tight brown-corduroy skirt and white plastic boots. I couldn't stop my eyes from straying to her middle. *Easy, girl,* I told myself, *don't borrow trouble. We'll know for sure by Monday.* I didn't think I could stand to wait three more days, but I knew there wasn't any choice.

The phone rang at two that afternoon. I set down the shirt I was mending for Jake and wasn't at all surprised to hear Libby's trembling voice.

"Mother, will you please come get me and Rachel? I want her to spend the night. Her mother already said it was okay."

"I'll be right there." I hung up, ignoring Libby's tone. "Her mother" had always been "Aunt Dotty" before. Now it seemed both girls had chosen to blame Dot and Sam for splitting them apart. I grabbed the car keys and headed for the Chevy with a prayer that Jake would have to work late. He had enough trouble dealing with Libby's emotional tirades. I hated to think what he would do with two angry teenagers under his roof.

* * *

Jake came home on the dot of five. Libby and Rachel had been closeted in Libby's room for nearly three hours. If I had known what they were really up to, I'd have been a whole lot more concerned. As it stood, I was grateful things were relatively quiet.

When I called them out to dinner, they greeted Jake politely, cut their spaghetti into small pieces and took dainty little bites. They said, "Please pass the Parmesan" and "Thank you for the lovely meal." Then they excused themselves and retreated once again into Libby's room.

"Now what?" Jake looked baffled, like a traveler in a foreign country where everyone else is speaking a different language.

I leaned over and patted his knee. "Well, dear," I said, "I do believe we've just been snubbed."

Chapter
Eighteen

The girls appeared early Saturday morning, before I'd even cracked an egg into Grandma Eva's shallow porcelain bowl. It was one of the few things Mama had handed down to me, and it was perfect for making French toast.

"May I borrow the car, please?" Libby wore a pair of new blue jeans and one of her father's old white shirts with "I love Elvis" embroidered across the back. She and Rachel both carried bags with books and papers sticking out of the top.

I looked at the clock. "Don't you want some breakfast first? The library doesn't open until ten."

Libby shrugged. "I'm not hungry, and we have to stop by Rachel's first."

"Yeah," Rachel spoke up. "I'm baby-sitting the Mathers kids tonight"—she wrinkled her nose like she smelled a dirty diaper—"and Libby promised to help me, so we have to get our homework done now."

I studied their faces. They both looked rested, even though Libby was still a little pale. "Are you sure you should do so much today?" I tried to keep my tone neutral. "You have been sick, remember?"

Libby blanched and shifted from one foot to the other. "I'm

fine, Mother. We just need to borrow the car." There was an edge of impatience to her voice, and I thought for the thousandth time how Mama, or even Aunt Rose, would have smacked me for sassing like that.

I couldn't smack Libby, of course. It would only make matters worse. "The keys are in my purse." I nodded toward the dining-room table, where I'd left my handbag the night before, and plugged in the percolator for Jake's coffee. "Tell Dad bye for me." Libby's lips brushed my cheek, and the girls hustled out the door. I felt a flash of apprehension at her words, then brushed it away. She'd done so many strange things lately, this was just one more to add to the list.

I guess I should have listened to my instincts.

I called Dotty around noon to check on them. "They stopped by here for some of Rachel's things, then went to the library," she said. "I told them they could eat here before they went to the Matherses'."

* * *

The phone rang at three a.m. "Celia, it's Sam. Put Jake on the line."

"Sam? What's wrong?" Then it hit me that I'd never heard Libby come home. I felt a rush of fear, then an icy calm. "It's the girls, isn't it? Has there been an accident?"

"No. At least I don't think so. But the girls never showed up at the Matherses'. In fact, the Matherses never went out last night. Those girls must have known we wouldn't check until it was too late."

I heard the shuffle of Jake's slippers on the carpet and the alarm in his voice when he came back and said, "Libby's not in her bed."

"Neither is Rachel." I handed him the phone.

A few minutes later he scrambled into the slacks he'd taken off the night before and pushed his bare feet into a pair of tennis shoes. "Sam says there's fifty dollars missing from Dotty's purse, and all the pop bottles are gone from the garage. Looks like they've run away." He shook his head. "Rachel must really be upset about this move, but I can't understand Libby going along with her. I thought she was more levelheaded than that."

There may be another reason for Libby's going. I almost said it aloud, but now was not the time to bring up my suspicions.

He pulled on his jacket and grabbed the keys to the Impala. "Wait till I get my hands on that kid," he muttered. He kissed my brow. "Don't worry, babe, we'll find them. Sam already called the police. They won't get far."

I could hardly contain my urge to jump in the Impala with him, but we'd decided it would be best for Dot and me to stay put, in case the girls called or the police came up with something.

As soon as I heard the squeal of Jake's tires on the driveway, I rushed into Libby's room. Sure enough, her dresser drawers were practically empty. She'd taken all her personal things and the photograph of Jake in his Navy blues.

Libby had been only three weeks old when her father sent that picture home. "Show this to my baby girl," the note had read. "I want her to know her daddy, even if I can't be there." I nearly ruined the portrait with my tears, but I bought a frame the very same day and kept it on the dresser by her crib. When the war ended and Jake finally came home, Libby was two and had picked him out of a crowd of nearly three hundred sailors.

My heart lurched at the memory. Once again I knew the panic I had felt when I looked down to find my child missing. We found her right away, clinging to her father's neck, patting his cheek and chanting, "Daddy, Daddy," both of them grinning to beat the band.

"Oh, Lord," I cried, "if only it could be that easy now." I fell to my knees and buried my face in Libby's pillow. It smelled like Windsong and freshly shampooed hair.

A few minutes later the telephone interrupted my prayers. "Celia, has Jake left yet?" Dot's voice was calm, but she kept having to clear her throat.

"About ten minutes ago."

"Well, the police just called. They found your car. We gave them a description when Sam reported the girls missing. I wanted you to know. They'll be calling you next."

"Dotty, the girls . . . were they . . . ?"

"No sign of them or their things. Rachel had two suitcases; both of them are gone. Celia, they found the car at the airport. Where do those two think they're going? How far can they get on fifty dollars?"

San Francisco. As soon as the thought entered my head, I knew I was right. And they had more than fifty dollars. There was money missing from my bag too. Luckily, I had just done the grocery shopping, so it couldn't have been much, but I would bet it was enough to get them to San Francisco and Anne Marie.

I felt giddy with relief. "Of course," I shouted into the telephone. "I'm sure the girls are okay, but I have to hang up. I'll call you back, I promise." She must have thought I'd gone insane.

* * *

As it turned out, they never even boarded the plane. The clerk told them the next flight to San Francisco wasn't until six a.m. Then a security guard became suspicious of two young girls traveling alone at that time of night. While they sat dangling their heels in the waiting room, he checked with the police.

We learned all of this much later, of course. The girls confessed their plans to fly to San Francisco, surprise my brother Chuck and somehow con him into letting them stay.

"Why Chuck?" I asked when things had calmed down a bit. "Why not Anne Marie?"

Libby looked at me like I was crazy. "Uncle Chuck is cool," she said. "Aunt Anne would have called you right away."

Libby insisted she had gone along only to help Rachel, who was dead set against the move to Washington, D.C. "She needed me, Mom, I couldn't just let her go alone." Libby's sobs were real, but her spirit wasn't a bit contrite. I knew she was lying, and she knew I knew.

By the time we got the whole thing sorted out, we were all exhausted. Libby's pallor was alarming, and she ran to the bathroom twice before the night was through.

The Levis took a sullen Rachel home, and Jake made it clear that Libby would spend eternity in her room. When we were convinced that she would stay there, at least for the next several hours, we both crawled into bed and slept until Sunday afternoon.

Chapter
Nineteen

The air-raid sirens went off at two a.m. on Monday. The minute I heard that piercing whine, I gripped Jake's arm and shook him awake. "This is it," I said as calmly as I could. "Jake, get up, we're under attack. You get Libby and I'll get the radio." I jumped out of bed and grabbed the transistor radio from the top shelf of the closet.

"Celia, calm down. It's probably just a test." Jake's voice was thick with sleep. "Even if it isn't, we've got no choice but to stay put."

"It can't be a test. They do that the first Saturday morning of the month, and at nine a.m., not in the middle of the night. I knew we should have built a shelter. We could have done it last summer. The Fergusons did, but it's so small. Maybe we should send Libby down there."

Jake had opened the window and was peering up and down the street. "All the lights are still on. I thought you were getting the radio."

"I have it, but it isn't working. The batteries must be dead."

"Oh, for Pete's sake." Jake flipped on the electric radio by the bed. Bob Dylan was singing "A Hard Rain's Gonna Fall," and on the next station a seductive female voice advised us that all her men wore English Leather.

Then, as abruptly as it had begun, the siren stopped.

"See, I told you, false alarm." Jake yawned and headed for the bathroom.

"What's going on?" Libby poked her head out of her room.

Jake patted her arm. "Go back to bed, sugar, nothing's going on. Your mother just thought we were under nuclear attack." He chuckled and shut the bathroom door.

"Mom?"

Libby looked so young and vulnerable standing there half asleep in her shorty pajamas. So many times she had stood in that very spot, clutching her beloved teddy bear, needing comfort from a tummy ache or some bad dream. I wanted to gather her in my arms now and hold her like I had when she was five.

I reached out and stroked her cheek. "It's all right, hon. False alarm. You can go back to sleep."

"Okay. 'Night."

She was seventeen. She could tuck herself back in.

When we climbed back into bed ourselves, Jake pulled me close and curled himself around my back, snuggling spoonlike into a comfortable position. "Are you all right, babe?" His warm breath stirred my hair and tickled my ear.

"I'm fine," I lied. "I'm sorry I woke you."

"I would never have slept through all that racket anyway." He put his arm over my waist. "I'll get new batteries for the radio tomorrow."

His breathing evened. I knew I'd never sleep. For one awful moment I was disappointed that it hadn't been the real thing. Then we wouldn't have to face the doctor's report today. I squeezed my eyes shut. *Oh, God, how could I even think such a thing?*

Scraps of Scripture verses tugged at my mind: "Cast all your care upon him, for he careth for you . . . Be careful for nothing

. . . Trust in the Lord . . ." If what I suspected was true—if our Libby was pregnant—we'd need all of God's strength to see us through.

* * *

Libby didn't even make an effort to go to school later that morning. So when the doctor's office called, we were able to go right in.

"I'm sure it's nothing, Mrs. Freeman," the nurse assured me. "We just need to repeat one test. It should only take a few minutes." I didn't have the nerve to ask which test.

Libby fidgeted all the way home, checking her makeup in the mirror, jiggling her foot, trying to avoid my eyes. Her own eyes were bright with unshed tears, and I knew I couldn't avoid a confrontation much longer—for her sake as well as mine.

"Where are we going?" She sounded alarmed when I pulled off onto Valley Boulevard instead of Wells Street.

"I thought you might want a Wild Onion Burger for lunch. We can eat in the car."

It was just 11:30 on a school day, and the drive-in restaurant was almost deserted. I ordered a burger and fries and a chocolate malt. Libby settled on fries and a lemon Coke. "Hamburger doesn't sound good right now," she grimaced and unconsciously placed her hand over her stomach.

I took a sip of the creamy malt and gathered my courage. "Libby, we need to talk," I said gently. "Is there something you want to tell me?"

She looked alarmed, and for a minute I thought she would choke on a fry. "No!" she shouted and swung toward the window. When she turned back, the tears were spilling down her cheeks. Still, she protested. "There's nothing to tell. Why can't you leave me alone?"

The anger in her face almost made me back away. But there was fear there too—and a desperation I hadn't seen since I was eleven, when Mama was pregnant and sick with the baby that died.

"Because I love you." As soon as the words were out, I felt surrounded by a cocoon of peace.

Libby must have felt it too. "Oh, Mom," she cried, "I'm so scared. Please, can we go home?"

* * *

By the time the doctor called that afternoon, I'd already heard most of Libby's story.

"It only happened once, I swear. How could I be pregnant when it only happened once?"

I cringed. I hadn't talked with Libby much about the facts of life. She'd learned most of what she needed to know in school, and I'd always thought we should wait until she became engaged to talk about man and woman relations. No one had ever talked to me. Aunt Rose had tried when Jake and I declared our intentions, but it was so uncomfortable for her, and for me, that I'd decided to wait until Libby came to me with questions. Obviously, that had been the wrong decision.

It turned out she'd been seeing Miguel all along, but she didn't confess to that right then. Rachel spilled those beans when Dotty was fishing for truth about the baby-sitting job. Rachel let something slip, and when Dot threatened to confiscate her diary, she confessed that Miguel had been visiting Libby at the Matherses' almost every afternoon until he went back to Mexico last July.

"No wonder she was so happy to go to San Francisco and turn those kids over to Rachel for the rest of the summer," I said when Dot was through.

"And no wonder Rachel couldn't handle the job," Dotty added. "She swears Libby and Miguel couldn't have done much over there. Those little monsters were too demanding. If anything, I would think it should have scared him off. Maybe he does love her, Celia. Have you thought about that?"

Jake and I didn't consider that until much later, when there were so many hard decisions to make. That Monday afternoon, Libby was so scared she didn't know how she felt about Miguel.

"I didn't hear from him for a while. Then I got a letter saying he was in Mexico with his family, and that he and Uncle Dave were coming here for the week between Christmas and New Year's. I couldn't say anything, Mom. You know Daddy would have made me stay with Nana Rose, and I just had to see Miguel. Grandma Freeman didn't know they were coming till they got there."

I was sure that was true. Jake's Ma would have surely said something if she had known.

"Everyone was sad on New Year's Eve," Libby continued, "because it had been a year since Grandpa died. Sara June and Grandma cried. Then Uncle Dave and Miguel came by with paper horns and ginger ale and said we were going to have a party. They brought a stack of records too, and Uncle Dave and I taught Aunt Sara to do the Twist. At midnight we sang 'Auld Lang Syne' with Dick Clark on TV." She grinned at the memory; then her smile faded. "When Grandma and Aunt Sara went to bed, Uncle Dave mixed some vodka with his ginger ale. Miguel didn't want any, but I did."

I couldn't hold my tongue. "Liberty Jane Freeman! You mean to tell me Dave let you drink vodka?"

She hung her head. "No. It was all my fault, Mom. Uncle Dave said, 'No way,' but when he was on the phone, I sneaked some anyhow."

"Oh, Libby."

"Uncle Dave had to go out for a while," she went on. "He told Miguel he'd pick him up in an hour and to be ready because they had to hustle." She sighed. "I didn't realize he meant they had to leave again."

Libby's voice grew quieter, more hesitant. "Miguel and I were dancing slow. I sneaked a couple more sips of Uncle Dave's drink, we sat down on the sofa and . . . it just happened." She began to sob. "I thought I loved him. I didn't even think . . . Just that once, and now I'm going to have his baby, and he's gone."

I wanted to shake her.

Her voice grew stronger until she was almost shouting. "Uncle Dave was being so cool. He told Grandma he'd saved up enough to pay Daddy back for the money he took. But when Daddy called, he sounded so mean. It must have made Uncle Dave change his mind. Now they're gone, and I'll probably never see Miguel again."

I couldn't let the last part go. "Liberty Jane, don't you dare blame your father for any of this. He's never had a thing to do with Dave's decisions, except to try and help him straighten out his life."

Libby looked shocked. "I didn't say it was his fault. But Uncle Dave knows he's mad. I guess he just got scared."

Dave scared? I didn't think so. But Jake's brother's reasons for fleeing back to Mexico were not the issue.

I handed Libby a tissue and put my arm around her. When she didn't pull away, I held her close and let my own tears flow. Just a few days ago I'd been crying like this with my best friend. When would the tears ever end?

Not in this life, sweetheart, I heard Mama whisper through the years. *Tears are God's way of washing away our pain.* I couldn't remember when she'd said it, but the words rang true.

After a while we drew apart and mopped our faces. "We'll work this out, darling, one step at a time. Unfortunately," I said, "the next step is to tell your father."

"He'll hate me, won't he, Mom?"

"Your father could never hate you. He'll be disappointed. But I know he'll do everything he can to help."

"Will you tell him? Please, I just can't. It was hard enough to tell you."

I nodded. *Lord, help me.* It wouldn't be easy, but somehow I'd have to find a way.

Chapter
Twenty

I decided to tell Jake after dinner, when he was relaxed and Libby had gone to her room. "Maybe he'll wait until tomorrow to talk," I told her. Jake liked to deal with problems right away, "before they get blown out of proportion." But this time I would suggest he take some time to think it over.

He walked through the door right at five o'clock, kissed my cheek and swiped his finger through the mashed-potato bowl. "Did you watch the launch today? They're suppose to replay it on the evening news." He headed straight for the living room and flipped on the TV.

The launch! In all the fuss with Libby, it had completely slipped my mind. I dried my hands on a dish towel and hurried into the living room.

"Libby," Jake called, "come watch this." I froze, but he was too distracted to notice she didn't answer.

The film was astounding: the rocket standing upright like a giant silver bullet on its launching pad, smoke billowing like stage fog around the bottom. But this wasn't a play. You could feel the tension in the air, see it in the faces of the military person-nel gathered at the site. They flashed a picture of the astronaut in his spacesuit fiddling with the dials on the control board.

You could hear the pride and excitement in the newscaster's voice when he said, "The United States made history today as Lieutenant Colonel John Glenn blasted off in Friendship 7 for the first manned space flight to orbit the earth."

Then the countdown began: "Ten ... nine ... eight ..." Flames shot up around the craft, and I gasped as the rocket moved slowly upward, piercing the sky with its needle-sharp nose. "Liftoff! We have liftoff!" And the crowd began to cheer. The craft turned toward its course, a sonic boom split the air, and the rocket shot into orbit.

Jake yelled. "Wow, did you see that, Celia?" And I realized I'd been holding my breath.

"In other news ..."

I smelled the meatloaf and hurried to snatch it from the oven. The last thing I needed was a burned dinner.

Ten minutes later Jake followed me to the kitchen. "Mmm, something smells good." He pecked my cheek, pulled out his chair and settled at the table. "Looks like they finally got a ruling on that segregation issue. After all the violence and bloodshed, Negroes no longer have to sit in the back of the bus."

"I'm glad." I forced a smile and set the meatloaf and potatoes on the table.

Jake nodded. "So am I. This is a free country. They should be allowed to sit anywhere they want." He unfolded his napkin and set it in his lap. "Of course, a bunch of hot-headed rednecks are protesting, throwing punches at the police. They carted at least five of them off to jail. Hi, pumpkin," he greeted Libby as she slid into her seat. "Feeling better?"

She managed to nod and smile, and Jake bowed his head to ask the blessing. He had just said "Amen" when the doorbell rang.

"I'll get it." He motioned for us both to sit and tossed his napkin on the table. It landed in the gravy, and I hurried to fish it out before it soaked up the entire bowl.

Libby just sat and stared at her food.

"Heaven help us. What are you doing here?" Jake's voice could have stopped a freight train.

"It's nice to see you too, Jake." The reply was sugar-sweet. "I've come to take charge of my cousin, of course."

Libby's head snapped up, and I hurried into the living room before the skirmish could escalate into all-out war. "Mary Margaret, what a nice surprise! Here, let me take your coat. Don't just stand there, darling." I urged Jake back toward the kitchen. "Your food's getting cold. You're just in time for dinner, M."

My voice had risen to a shrill squeak. I was sure I sounded like the witch cajoling Dorothy, but I couldn't stop myself. "Libby, look who's here," I said brightly. "Please help Daddy pull the table out and set another plate."

I flung Mary Margaret's coat into the entry closet, pushed the door closed with my foot and propelled her into the kitchen. I intended to deposit her onto the extra kitchen chair an get right on with dinner. Some say music can soothe a savage. I believe a good meal serves the same purpose. It had always worked with Jake, anyway.

Mary Margaret pulled away from me at the kitchen door and headed straight for Libby. "Hi, baby, I came as soon as I could."

Libby threw a look of panic in my direction, let out a sob and hurled herself into my cousin's arms.

* * *

It was springtime in Southern California, 1962. My baby, my seventeen-year-old daughter, was pregnant out of wedlock, but it was Mama's face that stalked my dreams. Mama, lying limp and still across her bed in Pike, Nevada, back in 1933. Mama, looking so fragile in her pink silk robe, with her paste-white skin and tear-reddened eyes, running to the bathroom and turning the water on full force so we wouldn't hear her being sick.

"Please watch the little ones for me, Cissy. Mama has to go lie down."

Mama, bent weeping over the tiny flower-draped coffin by a freshly dug grave up on Harris Hill.

* * *

Jake wouldn't talk about it for almost three days. He didn't rant and rave or make threats against Miguel, as I expected him to. Instead, after I convinced Mary Margaret to take Libby out for a Coke while I told Jake Libby's story, he buried his face in his hands for a full ten minutes, then kissed me hard and headed out the door. "I have to think, Celia. I'll be back."

He did come back. Every night around eleven. Always clean and calm and sober. His skin held an earthy smell of pitch and pine and dew-wet grass. I knew right away where he had gone.

Bear Lake had always been a hideaway for us—a place where promises were made and broken dreams mended. The pine-scented air, the spongy ground, the silence broken only by an egret's cry and wavelets lapping gently at the shore. A balm to soothe the shattered spirit.

How I envied him. I wanted more than anything to go with him and forget our troubles for a while. But he needed to be alone to sort things out. And Libby needed me. Her troubles could not be solved by a vacation in the mountains, no matter how tranquil the spot.

Mary Margaret had the grace to apologize for her intrusion. "Celia, I had no idea Jake didn't know. Libby's letter sounded so desperate. She was scared to death, and I was afraid she'd try something stupid. I knew you and Jake would be too shook up to think clearly."

"M!"

"All right." She held up her hand. "I'm sorry. But do you have any idea what some of these girls do? My best friend's daughter let some fool use a coat hanger on her."

"A coat hanger? You mean—?" I suddenly felt ninety years old and had to sit down on the sofa. I was glad Libby had finally cried herself to sleep.

She nodded. "These are the sixties, Celia. Abortions happen all the time. Usually in some back alley, with—"

"Stop!" I pointed toward the bedroom. "I don't want to hear anymore. Besides, Libby would never do a thing like that."

Mary Margaret shrugged. "You never know. My friend's daughter lived, but she'll never have another child. She was one of the lucky ones."

I sank back into the cushions and closed my eyes. I felt heartsick, exhausted and terribly alone.

* * *

When Jake finally called a family meeting, he was rational and calm. But I could feel the fire that fed his pain, and I was glad that Miguel was not around. It wasn't exactly an inquisition with bright lights and the third degree. More like a pretrial session of questions and answers, where the lawyer determines what track to take. I wondered if Jake had been talking to Sam.

Libby sat trembling in a comfortable chair by the window, while Jake sat on the edge of the sofa, elbows on his knees, hands clenched together just inches from his chin.

"Are you sure this Mex kid is the father?"

"Jake!"

"Daddy! His name's Miguel. I told you . . ."

"All right, all right." Jake lowered his head, inhaled, then looked up again. "Does he know?"

"No." Tears had formed in Libby's eyes, but she brushed them away. "He's in Mexico. His family lives there, but I don't know how to find them."

"That can't be too hard. What's his last name? I'm sure he can't support you, but he should take some responsibility for this."

I had tried to stay in the background, to let my husband handle this, but I couldn't just sit still and let him drive our daughter back into hysteria. I sat forward next to Jake and reached for her hand. "Libby, honey, do you love him? More important, does he love you?" I looked at Jake. "Lots of girls get married at seventeen, and Miguel is older, close to Dave's age."

As soon as I said it, I could have bitten my tongue. But Libby stepped in before her father could say a thing. "He's twenty-one. And I don't know, Mom." She buried her face in her hands. "I don't know if I love him. But he can't love me, or he wouldn't have run off with Uncle Dave."

There was flint in her tone, the same determination I'd heard so often in my mother's voice and knew to be in mine as well. People often thought Mama was weak because she fled inside herself where her troubles couldn't get her. She ran away, yes, but it was a choice she made—a selfish one, but her own decision nonetheless. "Celia." Jake's face had turned a sickly gray. "How can you even suggest that? The kid lives in Mexico. Marriage is out of the question."

Libby sat up straight. "Don't worry about it, Daddy. I'm not going to marry him. But it's not because his family lives in Mexico. It's because he—he just walked away."

For the first time since this whole mess started, I began to think we might survive.

Chapter
Twenty-one

March was a quiet month. A going-through-the-motions time, when little was accomplished and few decisions made.

When Mary Margaret realized we were not going to torture our daughter and that Libby had no intention of aborting her unborn child, she retreated to San Diego with promises to keep mum and admonishments to "call me if you need me."

"You know," she whispered when Jake was out of hearing range, "she can always stay with me. I looked after you when you were preggers. I can take care of Libby too."

We kept the news from the rest of the family as long as we could. And Libby managed to spend a few more weeks at school. Dotty and Sam had sworn Rachel to secrecy, with a promised penalty of life in her room if she dared tell a soul.

We talked to Libby about finding a loving family to adopt the baby. She didn't want to make that decision just then, although it was clear her father felt there was no other decision to be made. I prayed that neither Libby's choices nor mine and Jake's would be selfish ones. We had a child to think of here. A tiny human being who had no say in our decisions, but whose entire life would be affected by them.

"His last name is Flores," I complained to Dotty. "How on

earth do you find someone named Flores in Mexico? Especially when we don't even know what town. It's like trying to find a Johnson somewhere in Sweden."

"Maybe it's better that way, honey. It's unlikely they'd get married. Why not look at it as one less problem to deal with?"

I sighed. "You're right. We have enough trouble right now. We'll have to tell the family soon, and I have an appointment with Libby's school counselor tomorrow."

* * *

The vice principal at San Gabriel High, a man named Martin Caruthers, crouched behind a huge brown-metal desk strewn with file folders and at least twenty copies of *El Matador,* the school paper. He reached to shake my hand and pointed to a chrome and leather chair in front of the desk. "Have a seat— er, Mrs. Freeman?"

As I nodded and backed into the chair, I felt strangely like a child who'd been sent to the principal's office for misbehaving. I drew a deep breath to steady my nerves and explained the reason for my visit.

He cleared his throat and looked everywhere but into my eyes. "I'm sorry, Mrs. Freeman, but it's school policy that girls who become—er, in the family way cannot attend classes. A bad influence, you know." He yanked a pencil from behind his ear and tapped the desk to make his point. "Education is a privilege; we can't condone that kind of behavior, now can we?"

I felt an overpowering urge to kick him in the shins, but I kept my feet under control. "Why can't she finish out the year at home? Surely her teachers could send home reading material, and I could monitor tests."

"My dear lady, that's out of the question. In any case, your daughter has mostly elective classes." He studied the transcripts in his hands. "Let's see: choir, drama, P.E. History is the only hard subject she has. What a pity, such a good student too.

Ah, well . . ." He shrugged, stood and extended his hand. "My sympathy to you and your husband, Mrs. Freeman. If it were my daughter, I would see to it she married right away. But then, of course, there are always extenuating circumstances."

Thank God, Libby is not his daughter, I thought as I hurried out the door.

* * *

Aunt Rose went to pieces when she heard the news. Then she and Uncle Edward rallied with heartfelt prayers and loving gestures, including an offer to keep Libby until the baby was born.

"That way," Aunt Rose explained, "she will still be with family, but sheltered from any gossip or ridicule."

I began to see that Mary Margaret and Aunt Rose were right. When Libby's condition became obvious, there would undoubtedly be some who would perpetuate the scandal: loose tongues tipped with whiplash words. The sisters Livermore and Waggington, our church gossips, would be the first to cast stones.

Then I thought of Mr. and Mrs. Ferguson down the street. They had actually moved out of town and sent their seventeen-year-old daughter away. She'd returned just a few years ago with a four-year-old son. Jake and I didn't know them very well—they'd spurned our attempts to be neighborly—but just knowing that someone else had gone through the same ordeal was strangely comforting.

* * *

I wasn't there when Jake told his mother. "She cried," was all he would say when I asked how it went.

She was still crying when she called me the next day.

"It's all my fault," she sobbed. "I should have made the boys go away and seen Libby up to bed myself."

I gripped the receiver and tried to think of something comforting to say. The truth was, I'd been thinking the same thing.

I had to ask myself whether I would have gone off to bed leaving a young girl alone with two hoods—even if one of them was her uncle.

That, I thought, *is precisely what would have made her feel it was okay.*

"Dave was there, Mother Freeman. You couldn't have known he'd spike the drinks, then go off and leave them alone."

She sniffed, and I could hear her blow her nose. "Sara June and I were right upstairs. John was there when I went to bed. He must have left right after Brian and Pam."

"John and Brian were there too?"

"Land, yes. I had the whole crew, except for Anne Marie and Sara's Steven, and you and Jake, of course. Delbert would have loved it. He so enjoyed a good New Year's Eve party." She was sobbing again. "I don't understand what made Davy run off like that. He'd brought the money to pay Jake back—said he was going to settle down and get a job."

And you believed him? I didn't voice the thought; she had enough grief without me maligning Dave. Anyway, Jake did enough of that for both of us. I didn't say anything about the money in the well either. His mother hadn't mentioned it since the day Jake and his brothers had found the empty can. In fact, she'd made it clear the subject was off limits, just like Jake's brother Tim who'd been killed in the war. That had been nearly twenty years ago, and we still couldn't mention his name in her presence.

"Please don't blame yourself." My voice sounded stiff, and I deliberately softened it. "It was Libby's mistake, and it could have happened anywhere." I hung up and realized that was true. If Libby and Miguel had wanted to be together badly enough, they would have found a way.

That thought helped me with my own "if onlys": If only we hadn't gone to Hawaii. If only we had left Libby with Aunt

Rose. If only I had checked up on her when she was baby-sitting at the Matherses' and realized she'd never severed her relationship with Miguel.

Jake blamed Dave, of course. "That bum takes to trouble like a rat to cheese. If I get my hands on him . . ." He left the rest unsaid, which was just as well. I was sure he'd do his best to track down Miguel and make him own up to his actions, but he didn't even try. "I don't want that kid anywhere around here, Celia. God help me, but he'd better stay in Mexico where he belongs."

Although he tried, Jake couldn't even face Libby after the first interview. I felt like a moderator at a political debate. "Tell Libby this," Jake would say. "What does Daddy mean by that?" Libby would ask.

"Daddy hates me, doesn't he?" she asked one day toward the end of April.

"Liberty Jane, how can you say such a thing? Of course your father doesn't hate you. He loves you very much." I handed her the cotton smock I'd just made to go with her maternity shorts. She was barely showing yet, but it wouldn't be long before she wouldn't be able to wear her normal things.

"Well, he has a funny way of showing it. When he's home at all, he won't talk to me. He hides behind the paper whenever I come into the room."

She was right. He had been going early to the shop and staying until well after Libby and I had eaten dinner. When he did come home he barely said two words to anyone, just read the paper or watched TV.

"Give him time, honey," I said. "He has to deal with this in his own way." I knew it was a lame excuse for Jake's behavior, but I didn't know what else to say. He wouldn't share his pain with me either. I felt caught between the two people I loved the most, and I couldn't do a thing for either of them.

Libby held the smock up to her chin and looked in the mirror. "It's pretty, Mom, but isn't it kind of big?"

I laughed in spite of the situation. "Just wait a month or two. You'll grow into it."

Libby didn't even smile. She turned and sat gingerly on the edge of my bed, tapping her foot and looking anywhere but at me. "Mom?" she said. "I want to go away. Rachel is leaving in two more weeks, and Carol's busy with her boyfriend. I won't have any friends here."

There were tears in her eyes, and I knew some of her friends were already whispering behind her back. A few adults had even snubbed her. True, most of the people at church had been supportive, but last Sunday, after the service, Betty Furnace had marched up to Libby in the foyer and hissed, "Shame on you," right to her face. I'd seen her talking to Edna Livermore just before that, so it didn't surprise me any, but it certainly embarrassed us both.

Now I found myself facing the inevitable with a surprising sense of relief. "Well," I said as calmly as I could, "you know Aunt Rose would love to have you. She's offered several times, and you'd be close enough for us to visit."

Libby looked at the floor and shook her head. "Nana Rose is the greatest, but I couldn't stand it, Mom. Every time she and Papa Edward look at me, I can see how much I've hurt them." She straightened her back and looked me in the eye. "No. You said it's time I took some responsibility and made some good decisions. Well, I've made one."

I held my breath. What if she wanted to go to Mary Margaret's? Jake would have a heart attack and try to send her to some unwed-mothers home.

"I want to go to San Francisco." She fished in her pocket and handed me an envelope. "I want to stay with Aunt Anne. She says she'd like to have me. And since she's a nurse, I couldn't be in better hands."

I exhaled with relief.

That last line was straight from the letter she gave me. It was addressed to Mr. and Mrs. Jake Freeman and Libby, so I couldn't fault her for opening it first.

Chuck and I talked it over, and, if you and Jake are in agreement, Libby would be welcome here. I could help her through the pregnancy and delivery. One of my colleagues is an obstetrician. Chuck works mainly evenings, and he only lives a few blocks away, so he could be here if she needs him during the day. She'd be in good hands, I promise. Think about it. If you decide to send her, Chuck will mail her a ticket. Keep in mind she should come as soon as possible to get set up with the doctor and hospital.

The letter continued for several paragraphs, then ended with Anne's usual Spirit-filled wisdom: "I know this seems like the end of the world, but it isn't. Keep in mind that God has a plan for every life, including Libby's and this baby's. I just know he or she will be someone very special, in spite of the circumstances." It was signed, "Love and kisses, Anne Marie."

* * *

I handed Jake the letter with his cold roast beef and sat down next to him at the table.

"What's this?" He raised his eyebrows and unfolded the pages without waiting for an answer.

I gave him time to digest the suggestion, then spoke up. "I think it's a good idea. Anne and Chuck both love her, and she did so well with them this summer."

I expected him to insist we could take care of our own daughter, but he surprised me by agreeing right away. "Anne's right. She and Chuck seem to know her better than I do. Besides"— he looked right through me to the calendar on the wall by the telephone—"I think a few months' separation would be good for all of us." He finished his milk and pushed back from the table. "But you can tell Chuck that I'll buy the ticket."

That was April 25. On April 26 Ranger 4 crashed into the far side of the moon.

Chapter
Twenty-two

The warm April breeze stirred up the heady scent of jasmine
and the mock orange tree I had planted the summer before.

"Leave the window open, darling," I said to Jake as we got
ready to watch TV. "The fresh air feels good."

He shrugged and flipped the dial on the new Philco he'd
bought last October. *Wagon Train* had just started, but the first
half was interrupted twice with news. "Ladies and gentlemen,
we have just received word that Ranger 4, the first United
States lunar probe to reach the moon, has collided with its
target. Please stay tuned for further information."

"Good grief," I said, "what if there had been a human being
on board? That just goes to show they should quit fooling with
things best left to God."

Jake shook his head. "You don't know what you're talking
about, Celia. We have to explore the possibilities of space. You
can bet your boots the Russians are. Do you want to leave it
to them?"

He sounded irked, and I bit my tongue to keep from answering back. Maybe he had a point, I realized. Was I voicing my
own opinion or echoing Aunt Rose? *I'm getting stale,* I thought
for the thousandth time. *I've been so engrossed with family problems I haven't kept up with the times.*

The answer, as I saw it, was to go back to work. But every time I brought the subject up, Jake was quick to point out the reasons I shouldn't. "Libby needs you" was his favorite. What he didn't say was "I need you." If he had, I might have been content to stay at home.

The roar of a motorcycle turning the corner of Lafayette and Wells brought me out of my reverie. My heart jumped and my first thought was, *Oh, Lord, please don't let it be Miguel.* I glanced at Libby's bedroom door. She had turned in half an hour ago, but she might still be awake.

Jake followed my gaze. I could tell he was thinking the same thing. His face had darkened, his eyes narrowing to dark-brown slits.

The roar increased in volume and speed, and I thought it would rush on by. But at the last minute the driver geared down and, tires squealing, skidded to a stop in the driveway. When he bent to set the kickstand, all I could see was a head of dark, wavy hair, a black leather jacket and silver-studded hobnail boots.

Jake's face was calm, but his voice was hard and sharp as steel. "Stay put, Celia, I'll handle this." He was out the door and on the porch before I could think to disobey.

The cyclist didn't hesitate. He strode across the lawn and, as he came up even with the window, turned his head to glance inside.

Dave.

My stomach flipped. I didn't know whether to be relieved or more afraid.

They were talking then, their voices low. I could only hear snatches of the conversation, so I ignored Jake's warning and went to the door.

"Wait!" Dave's tone was sharp with frustration. "I came to talk to you, man. And this time you will listen," he said, swearing loudly.

I yanked open the door, but neither of them seemed to hear me. Dave had his fist tangled in the front of Jake's T-shirt, and my husband's face was a grotesque mask of barely controlled anger. If I didn't know better, I would have said he hated his brother right then.

"Watch your mouth." Jake spit the words, like darts thrown at a target. "And get your hands off my shirt."

To my surprise, Dave's grip relaxed and he stepped back. But his face didn't soften, and he didn't turn away. Instead he reached into the pocket of his jacket, drew out an envelope, grabbed Jake's hand and slapped it into his open palm. "Here. I pay my debts.

"Go ahead, count it," he said when Jake didn't move to open the envelope. "It's all there, every last cent I took from the till."

Jake's mouth twitched. "What about the rest of it?"

Dave looked surprised, "Rest of it? I told you, man, it's all there . . ." His eyes narrowed, and I knew he understood. His hands dropped to his side, and for one short moment he looked so sad and vulnerable, like the Davy I had known as a little boy—full of mischief, yet penitent when caught. Then his face hardened again. "So you still think I took Ma's money." He shook his head. "What've I got to do to make you understand? I didn't take that money from the well!"

He was shouting now, cursing. I saw the curtains flutter at the Jeffersons' window across the street and was afraid they might call the police. I opened the screen door and stepped outside. "Come in here, you two, before you have the whole neighborhood in an uproar." I used the same stern tone I would use with misbehaving children or a naughty dog.

It worked. Dave turned first and was in the living room before Jake could get another word out. Jake followed reluctantly, giving me a look that cursed my interference. If he had been a cat, he would have hissed at me. The image made me want to laugh, and I took my time fastening the screen and closing the front door.

When I turned back, they were still standing head to head in the living room. I decided to try again. "Sit down, Dave. Do you want something to drink? I have Coke, iced tea or coffee."

"If we don't have any beer," Jake sneered, "I doubt if he's interested."

Dave smiled and flopped down on the sofa. "I'll take a Coke, Cissy. The bottle's fine."

Jake had no choice but to sit, and when I got back with the drinks, they were perched on opposite ends of the couch like petulant schoolboys. Jake ignored the drink, so I set it on the coffee table next to the unopened envelope and took my iced tea to the straight-backed chair in the corner by the window.

There was no sound from Libby's room. Either she was asleep and unaware we had a visitor, or she was afraid to face both her father and uncle at the same time. I had to believe she was asleep. If she knew Dave was here she would be out in a flash, thinking he might have a message from Miguel.

Dave took a long swallow of his Coke and cleared his throat. "Think what you want about the money, man. This is all I took, right here." He tapped the coffee table with his finger. "I'm giving it back"—he paused for effect—"with interest."

Something in his tone made me lean forward in my seat.

Jake's head snapped up. "What do you mean, with interest?"

Dave examined his knuckles, picking at the rough skin with a thumbnail. "I mean, I know how to find that scum Miguel." His mouth tightened. When he looked up at me, I could have sworn his eyes were bright with tears. He looked quickly away.

Jake's shoulders stiffened, and he sat stone-still waiting for his brother to go on.

Dave stood and turned to face him. "Ma told me what he did

to Libby."

Jake winced, but didn't lift his eyes.

"Look, man. She's just a kid. I swear I didn't know what was going on. He talked about her like she was his sister or something."

"They'd been seeing each other for over a year, and you expect me to believe you didn't know it?"

"Believe what you want," Dave shot back. "You will anyway. You're a bullheaded bigot, just like our old man."

Jake jumped to his feet.

"Jake, don't!" I cried out.

But Dave wasn't giving Jake a chance to hit him. He grabbed his gloves and backed toward the door. "Believe this, big brother: I'll find Miguel. And when I get through with the little maggot, you won't have to worry about him bothering Libby again."

"Uncle Dave!" Libby's cry was like a death wail, and for an instant everyone froze. She stood in the hallway wrapped in a terrycloth robe, her hair in tangled strands, her eyes swollen, her lips white. "Uncle Dave," she said again, "don't. Please don't hurt Miguel."

Dave jerked his eyes away from hers and bolted out the door.

"Libby, go back to bed," Jake said evenly, keeping his eyes on Dave.

Libby ignored him and ran to the window, yelling, "Uncle Dave, come back! It was my fault, please don't hurt him." I pulled her into my arms and let her sob against my breast, as she had when she was little and had skinned her knee. I wanted to kiss the hurt, bandage the wound and make it all go away.

We huddled there while the eleven-o'clock news flashed pictures of the rocket that had crashed into the moon, and Hugh Downs announced the beginning of *The Tonight Show.*

Jake moved to the porch and stayed long after the roar of his brother's motorcycle faded into the night.

Chapter
Twenty-three

We said goodby to the Levis the first Saturday in May. Actually Sam had left three weeks before and driven his Packard all the way to D.C. Then he'd flown back to help Dotty with the luggage and supervise the loading of the moving van.

Even at six a.m., L.A. International was packed from the parking lot to the runways. We grabbed two empty tables in one of the cafeterias, then sent Jake and Sam through the line with orders for coffee, sweet rolls, cocoa and milk.

Dot and I had already promised to write, and we assured each other we were only a phone call away. "We'll visit at least once a year," she had promised, "and you can come out after the baby's born. Everyone should see the capital at least once." Neither of us wanted to break down in public, so we stared at our coffee cups and pretended to be content listening to the children babbling at the other table. The boys were particularly excited; after hours of extra homework and final exams, they had been released from school a good four weeks early.

"Well, I'm glad we're moving." Rachel's voice rose over the din. Dotty lifted her head slightly, careful not to look in that direction. I paid attention too. Rachel had fought this move from the start; why the sudden change in attitude? From the corner of my eye, I could see she was shredding her napkin into an ashtray and addressing her comments to Libby, who sat pale and solemn across from her.

"You're splitting to Frisco, and Carol thinks she's such hot stuff going steady with Ritche Conway." She leaned forward, and I had to strain to hear the next few sentences. "I'll bet you didn't know Carol's got this boss job serving espresso at the Back Door. You know, that place where Ritche plays the bongos." She giggled and leaned closer to Libby. "Her mother thinks she's waiting tables at the Square Burger."

Dotty's head was in her hands, and I couldn't tell if she was laughing or crying. I was trying to sort out how much truth was in the tale and whether or not I had an obligation to tell Carol's mother.

Just then the men returned, putting an end to Rachel's conversation.

"Here you go, crew." Sam's levity sounded forced. "If we eat all this, the plane will never get off the ground."

Dotty grimaced. "Sam, you promised, no airplane jokes. We're all nervous enough as it is."

He patted her shoulder and looked penitent while Jake handed me my coffee and bear claw, then plopped into the last vacant chair. "Man, what a crowd. And we have to do this again next weekend."

My spirits sank even further. It was true. Libby had reservations on next Saturday's flight to San Francisco. She had insisted on flying alone, and my brother Chuck had promised to pick her up at the airport.

As we finished our makeshift breakfast and escorted our best friends to the "holding pen," as Jake called it, I felt panic building in the pit of my stomach. The crowds pressed around us, and I found myself struggling to breathe.

Hugs all around. Promises coerced: "Be good." "Mind your

mother." "Say hello to the president." Forced laughter from everyone. From Jake to John, "Don't let the bedbugs bite." A strangle hug for both of us from Zeke. My head was spinning.

We elbowed our way back toward the terminal entrance. Libby kept hold of her father's arm. *As if he's walking her down the aisle,* I thought. I fought the dizziness all the way to the parking lot, then lost my breakfast behind the rear fender of a brand-new 1962 Mercury.

* * *

Aunt Rose dipped a washrag into cool water and sponged my head for the hundredth time. I reached again for the trash can by Mary Margaret's old bed, then lay back, exhausted, on the propped-up pillows.

"It's a good thing Jake brought you over here," Aunt Rose said. "It would be terrible if Libby got this awful flu." I tried to nod, but someone was pounding on my head with a rubber mallet. My tongue felt like a wad of cotton batting, and my skin hurt from my shoulders to my toes.

Aunt Rose tried to spoon-feed me broth and coaxed me to take water through a straw. By Friday night I could hold it down, but I was still too weak to go home.

Jake telephoned when he got home from work at six. "Thank God you're better." He sounded tired. "I've been worried about you, babe."

"What about tomorrow?" I had to say it twice before he understood my croaking voice.

"Tomorrow? Oh. Don't worry, I'll take Libby to the airport, then pick you up tomorrow afternoon. Just rest. I'll be sure she's safely on the plane." He paused, then whispered something like he was talking to himself. I couldn't be sure, but it sounded like "The rest is up to God."

* * *

Jake picked me up the next afternoon as promised. Aunt

Rose had fixed roast beef with carrots and potatoes. Jake ate heartily, as usual, but I stuck to Jell-O and an unbuttered roll.

"Are you sure you're okay?" I asked Aunt Rose as Jake helped me into the car.

"I'm fine, dear. Just tired. None of us has had much sleep this week."

Uncle Edward kissed my cheek, then wrapped his arm around Aunt Rose's shoulders. "Don't worry, sweetheart, Rosie has nursed this family for years. She never takes time to get sick herself."

His grin was contagious, and I smiled as Jake shook his hand and planted a kiss on Aunt Rose's cheek. "Thanks, Rosebud. You take care of yourself. We couldn't do without you."

*   *   *

I managed to keep up the laundry and cook dinner that next week, but with Libby gone there was really no reason to push myself. Jake came home every evening and helped me with the dishes. We watched TV for an hour or so, then crawled off to bed like candidates for an old folks' home.

By the third week in May my strength had returned and I was feeling restless. I'd received a letter from Dotty saying things were going well. "Sam's enthusiastic about his job, and the children all like the neighborhood. David has a library card, and Rachel is already talking about going steady with the boy across the street." Not a word about herself, but that didn't surprise me. I'd have to forage out her feelings on the phone.

Libby called to report the doctor's verdict: mother and baby were doing fine. Anne got on the phone and said Libby's color had improved and she was thriving in the cool ocean air.

"I wonder if it could have been the smog that was making her so sick," I told Jake that night. "It's been pretty thick here lately."

He just grunted, like he did whenever Libby's condition was

mentioned, and turned back to the TV and the second half of
Gunsmoke. Festus was twisting his hat in his hand and making
eyes at Miss Kitty, while Marshall Dillon lounged carelessly
against the hitching post in front of the saloon. I noticed he
always kept the handle of his gun in plain sight.

Florence called the next day. "Can you meet us for lunch
tomorrow, Celia? Stuart and I have a proposition for you." She
sounded so cheerful and eager, I didn't even hesitate.

"I'd love to. Twelve o'clock at the Central?"

"Make it eleven-thirty at the Coffee Mill. One of my students
is doing a poetry reading, and I promised I'd be there."

"A poetry reading? Are you serious?"

"Perfectly. Haven't you heard? This is the beat generation.
And as they say, it'll be a gas!"

I laughed and hung up. For the first time in months, I found
myself humming as I mixed the batter for a cake.

Chapter
Twenty-four

I drove into town in spite of the heat and the smog. The thought of standing shoulder to shoulder with other commuters on a crowded bus made my head start pounding all over again. By the time I parked and walked the six blocks to the café, I felt as wilted as the pansies someone had planted in front of Milo's Music Shop.

Flo was already at the table. She'd had her hair cut in one of those shorter, curly styles that made her look eighteen instead of almost twenty-seven. She jumped up and gave me a hug. "Hi, sis. Long time no see. Wow, you look like you could use a pick-me-up." She motioned to the waitress. "Bring my sister an espresso, please. Wait, make that two; here comes Stuart." She smiled and half-stood to wave him toward our table.

I felt the warmth of his hand on my shoulder and smelled his cologne. English Leather. I'd bought Jake a bottle for Christmas, but he hadn't used it yet. "Celia!" His lips brushed my cheek. "It's good to see you. I called the house last week and Jake said you were sick."

The concern on his face was genuine, and I felt my spirits rise a little. "I'm better, thanks. I've been much too lazy. I'm glad

Flo suggested lunch."

He smiled and pulled out his chair. "So am I," he said. "It's been too long."

Flo and I both ordered chicken salad sandwiches. Stuart ordered a hamburger, took a sip of his espresso, then grimaced. "I never could abide these things."

Flo looked wounded, but she recovered quickly. "I haven't said anything to Celia yet. I thought maybe you would want to ask her."

"Ask me what?" I took a sip of the mud-black liquid in the demitasse and tried not to make a face.

"Well." Stuart stretched his long arms in front of him, clasped his hands together, then bent them back, popping all ten knuckles at once. "How would you like to come to work for me?"

The lights flickered, then dimmed. Someone pounded out a beat on bongo drums, and a young man with shaggy hair and a half-grown goatee began to recite a poem.

I was too stunned to listen. *Me, work for Stuart?* I leaned over and whispered, "Since when do they let professors hire secretaries?"

"Not as a secretary," he whispered back. "As my research assistant."

The young poet bowed his head to a smattering of applause, and the overhead lights flashed on.

Florence turned her attention back to the table. "Stuart has a grant to do a study on adopted children and their parents. I told him with your experience at Children's Charities, you'd be perfect for the job." She looked at him and grinned. "I get to be a guinea pig. Chuck too, if he'll cooperate."

"You'll have to fill out an application," Stuart said to me as he pulled several sheets of paper from his briefcase and pushed them across the table. "University rules. But that's just routine.

Chapter Twenty-four

The job is yours if you want it."

Florence squeezed my arm. "Please say yes. It would be such fun having you around. And the hours are flexible." She glanced at Stuart. "You could take time off whenever you needed to . . . to be with Libby."

I felt my face go red. "I'll think about it," I said. I pushed aside the remains of my sandwich and glanced at my watch. "I really should go." I forced myself to look at Stuart. His eyes were full of compassion. I stood to leave. "I'll talk to Jake and let you know."

I turned and hurried to the car. Why should it bother me so that my sister had told Stuart Haley about Libby? Things like that were as impossible to keep quiet as thunder in a rainstorm. Yet somehow the fact that Libby's pregnancy was fast becoming common knowledge upset me almost as much as her condition itself.

"A prideful heart is an abomination to God." I could hear our pastor's admonishment as if it were yesterday. Actually it had been weeks since I'd been to church. If I were truthful, I'd have to admit it wasn't just because I hadn't been feeling good.

I realized I didn't want to face the looks of pity or disdain. And I didn't want to face the struggle going on in my own heart. *In fact,* I told myself as I unlocked the door and climbed behind the steering wheel of my car, *I don't want to have to deal with it at all.*

Yet I knew my denial wouldn't make Libby's condition go away. Was I wrong to send her off to Anne Marie? Was I asking someone else to handle what was my responsibility? My head began its pulsing ache from the back of my neck to my temples. I took the Garfield exit, stopped at the drugstore for aspirin and downed three with a lemon Coke. But when I got home, my ears were still ringing with the pain.

* * *

The headache subsided around nine o'clock. By the time we went to bed at ten, I felt I could think clearly enough to tell Jake about Stuart's invitation.

His body stiffened perceptibly when I mentioned going back to work, but he stayed silent and let me have my say. "It sounds like interesting work," I concluded. "It's only part time, but it would give me spending money and help to fill my day."

"If you needed more spending money, you could have come to me."

I raised up on my elbow. "Jake, that's not the point. And anyway, I didn't ask for this job, Flo and Stuart came to me."

"What's Flo got to do with it? Her only summer project is Jerry."

His face was little more than a shadow in the darkened room, but I could sense the clenched jaw and set lips. "Jake Freeman, if I didn't know better, I'd say . . . "

"Say what, Celia?" he said quietly.

I lay back against my pillow. "Are you jealous of Stuart Haley?" I tried to keep the humor out of my voice. "Because you have no reason—"

"Don't be ridiculous!" His protest was muffled by the sheet he pulled up to his nose as he turned away from me. "Take the job, if you want it that bad," he muttered. "It doesn't matter to me."

* * *

I dreamed we were at my old house on York Street, lying on our backs, side by side in the cool, damp grass behind the apple tree. We were not quite touching, but I could feel the motion of his arm as he plucked a clover stem to chew, and smell the heady earth-scent of his sun-warmed skin.

"Look there, Cissy." He pointed to a cloud. "A girl with a veil."

"A bride!" I could feel my face heat up, but the picture was so clear. "See the train on her gown? And that little cloud right there is her bouquet."

Jake turned on his side, his breath tickling my ear. "Is it you, Cissy? Are you the bride?"

His tone was so serious. I turned my head to see his face, and he was smiling down at me, a look of wonder in his eyes.

I was about to ask, "Do you want it to be me?" when I heard the doorbell ring. I called out to Mama, "Someone's at the door," but the sound grew louder, more persistent, and I knew she wasn't going to answer.

"Jake?" I came awake and felt the mattress bounce as he jumped to his feet.

"I'll get it; just lie still."

I turned my head and looked at the clock. Five-thirty a.m. *Who on earth?* Even as I swung my legs over the side of the bed and struggled into my robe, my dream lingered in my mind.

Chapter
Twenty-five

Jake was back before I could rub the sleep out of my eyes. "It's Brian. He says there's more trouble with Dave, and Ma's hysterical." He pulled on an undershirt and shoved his legs into a pair of ragged blue jeans. "Would you call Ron at home and get him to open the shop? Tell him I'll be there as soon as I can."

"Not on your life, Jake Freeman!" I was shocked by my own tone and lowered my voice. "I'll call, of course, but I'm going with you. Your mother might need me."

He didn't try to dissuade me. "Hurry up, then. We may have to drive her to the hospital. Brian thinks she needs a sedative."

Then why didn't he drive her himself? But I knew the answer. Since their pa died and Anne Marie went back to San Francisco, the rest of the tribe had turned to Jake for everything. As the oldest, it was up to him to solve every little problem and have all the answers. Poor Jake. No wonder he was always exhausted. Between his family's needs and Libby's problems, he must have felt like he was lugging a load of bricks around all day.

* * *

Ma's living room was neat as a pin except for a pile of discarded tissues on the floor next to the sofa, where she sat weeping and blowing her nose. John perched helplessly on the edge of his father's recliner. He looked relieved when he saw me, and lifted his hands in a what-do-we-do-now gesture.

I reached Ma's side the same time as Jake. Her face was as gray as the pile of wood ash in the fireplace, her white hair damp and matted to her clean pink scalp. She clung to Jake for dear life, while I put my fingers on her pulse. Her heartbeat quickened, then slowed as she drew herself up and blew into yet another tissue.

"My Jake." She patted his face, then turned to me. "I am so sorry to drag you out of bed like this, Celia, but our Davy's in trouble, and I don't know what to do."

Jake cleared his throat. "You better tell me what happened, Ma. Brian's version's pretty sketchy."

She was quick to explain. "Two men came knocking on the door at five in the morning. Liked to scare me to death. I wasn't going to answer it, but one called out he was the FBI and showed me his badge through the window. It looked real enough." She looked at Jake for approval. "Like on television, you know?"

Jake nodded his assurance and she continued. "They asked did David Freeman live here, and I said, 'Sometimes, but he's not here now.' Then they asked am I his mother. I told them yes, then asked, 'What's wrong?' and they said Davy's locked up in jail down in Mexico for beating up another man. 'Nearly killed him,' they said."

"He must have caught up with Miguel!" I sank back into the sofa.

Jake's face was grim. "Was it Miguel?"

He had to ask it twice before Ma nodded. "I expect it was. They said a Mr. Flores was in a hospital in Ensenada. If he dies, they said our Davy will be charged with murder." She buried her face in her hands and burst into a fresh barrage of tears.

* * *

Jake spent every spare minute for a week contacting authorities, trying to get his brother extradited back to the United States. "I wouldn't wish a Mexican jail on a pack of rats," was how he put it.

To make things worse, no one would tell us how Miguel was doing. All we knew for sure was that he hadn't died; at least the charges against Dave had not been upgraded to murder.

Brian surprised us by insisting he move back in with his mother.

"Jake," I asked that Saturday, as he was leaving to help Brian move his bed and stereo set, "why Brian? Wouldn't John be the more logical one?"

Jake tied a double knot on his tennis shoe. "Maybe. John's the only one not 'attached,' but he's also the most ineffective." He stood and tucked his T-shirt into his jeans. "You saw him at Ma's: he turns to putty in a crisis. And Lord knows this family has enough of those."

I moved in front of him, put my arms around his waist and laid my head against his chest. His arms came around me automatically, and we stood like that, his heartbeat slow and steady underneath my ear. I closed my eyes and, for a moment, felt at peace.

Jake's arms tightened, then released me. "I have to go, babe. Brian's waiting." He dropped a kiss on the crown of my head and hurried out the door.

* * *

We decided not to tell Libby until we knew more about Miguel's condition. We called, as usual, on Sunday afternoon and kept our conversation light. "You sound funny, Mom," she said at one point. "Is anything wrong?"

"I'm just tired, hon," I told her and put her father on the phone. They talked about the weather and what she'd had to eat that week. They never discussed her condition or anything about the future. It was as if they had an unspoken agreement to pretend she was just on another vacation visit with her Aunt Anne and Uncle Chuck.

Finally, after days of fretting and hours of unproductive phone calls, Jake played his last card. It turned out to be a trump.

"Where's the Levis' phone number?" he asked at eight o'clock Sunday night.

"In the black rotary file," I told him. "But darling, you can't call them now. It's eleven o'clock back there."

"I have to, Celia. Sam's my last hope. If no one else can get Dave home, maybe the assistant attorney general can."

Sam answered on the third ring. They talked for ten minutes and hung up without offering Dotty or me the phone. Jake looked glum. "He didn't sound too encouraging. Said he'd see what he could do, though. He'll get back to us in a day or two." He rubbed his hands over his face and back through his short-cropped hair. There were more than just a few strands of gray along the sides and at his temples.

So far I'd been able to keep gray pruned out of mine by having it cut every two months, but more showed up every day. I knew it wouldn't be long before I'd be making extra trips to the hairdresser for coloring. "We'll know we're getting old when we have to color our hair," Dotty and I used to joke. How could the years have passed so quickly?

Jake's loud sigh drew me back to the present. "Whew. I don't know about you, but I'm beat." He kissed my cheek. "I'm going to bed. I'll try not to wake you when I get up tomorrow."

I wanted to say, "Please wake me. Sit and have a cup of coffee with me, like you used to. Talk awhile, then smile a real smile and give me a real kiss goodby." But I didn't want to add to his burdens by acting like a disgruntled wife. Instead I hunted up

my Bible and read until my eyes were tired and I knew I'd be
able to fall asleep.

* * *

On June 1, 1962, the temperature hit ninety degrees by ten
a.m. I shut all the windows, turned on the cooler and stripped
down to my underclothes. There were dishes in the sink, and
the living room needed dusting, but I decided to read instead.
I covered Jake's vinyl recliner with a cotton sheet and turned
it toward the flow of water-cooled air.

My job with Stuart didn't start until the last week in June,
so I'd picked up a novel to help me pass the time. *Fail-Safe* was
the new bestseller about the accidental launch of a nuclear
strike against Russia. By page ten I had goosebumps in spite
of the heat. When the phone interrupted my concentration, I
was almost relieved.

"It all sounds so plausible," I told Aunt Rose. "Do you know
how easy it would be for something like that to really happen?"

"Now dear, don't get overwrought. It's this heat. We're roast-
ing out here, but at least we have clean air and a slight breeze."
She paused. "Why don't you and Jake come out this weekend?
It's been so long since we've had a really nice visit. I'll fix cold
chicken and potato salad. We can have a picnic on the patio."

I could tell by her voice that there was something besides
chicken on her mind. The words *nice visit* rang in my ear as
if she had shouted them. "Of course we'll come, Aunt Rose. It
will do Jake good to get away." I explained that Jake's mother
was doing better, now that Brian had moved in. We'd talked to
Libby Sunday, and she was feeling fine. No, we didn't know
how Miguel was doing, and there was still no word from Sam.
Then I hung up on the first phone call of a very busy day.

Chapter
Twenty-six

I had just fixed a bowl of cold cereal for my breakfast when the phone rang again. This time it was Brian's fiancée, Pam, and she was crying so hard I could hardly understand her.

Now what? I thought, and felt a sense of alarm. I hardly knew Pam. Why would she be calling me unless something had happened to Brian?

"Celia," she sobbed, "do you know what's gotten into Brian? He called last night and canceled the wedding, just like that! He said his mother needs him, and he has some personal problems he needs to work through. Personal problems! He's always talked things out with me before. He's changed so much since his father died. It's almost as if he feels guilty, as if he thinks it was his fault or something. Now this thing with Dave has him acting crazy."

I tried to hide my relief. At least Brian was alive and well. "Have you tried talking to him?" I asked gently.

"Yes," she sniffed. "He says he still loves me. He told me, 'I'd like you to wait, but I'll understand if you don't want to.' He'll understand! What a bunch of baloney! I'm the one who needs to understand." She was shouting now, and I held the phone away from my ear. "I'm going to get to the bottom of this. If

Brian Freeman thinks he can push me aside that easily, he's got another think coming!"

"Well, maybe you should just give him some time . . ."

"Thanks, Celia," she interrupted. "You've been a big help. We'll be sisters-in-law before you know it, or Brian's hide is toast!" The line clicked dead.

"Ha," Jake said when I told him about the conversation that night. "I guess good old Brian's met his match. It's about time someone lit a fire under him."

* * *

Jake dragged in about five-thirty. "It's one hundred degrees at the shop. We had two clients cancel because they didn't want to come out in it. I can't blame them." He shucked his clothes and sauntered toward the bathroom. "I'm going to shower. I hope you made something cool for dinner."

"There's tuna salad in the fridge." I'd already had a shower and forced myself into a pair of shorts and a faded cotton blouse. The cooler kept the living room bearable but hardly touched the rest of the house, so I set up two TV trays and poured tall glasses of iced tea.

We were halfway through our salads when the phone rang.

"Honestly, Jake, that's the fifth call today. Sometimes I wish we could just let it ring."

He flashed me a tolerant grin and went to answer the phone.

"Sam!" Jake's eyes lit up with hope. After he had listened a few minutes, a relieved smile spread across his face. He closed his eyes and sank into a straightback chair. "That's great, buddy. Thanks, I owe you one." He hung up.

"Dave's okay." He looked up at the ceiling as if it weren't there and heaven were in the open sky above us. "And, thank God, Miguel will live." I closed my eyes and added my thanksgiving to Jake's.

He came back to the sofa, picked up his fork and set it down again.

"When will Dave be home?" I asked.

"In ninety days. Well, more like seventy-five. If he decides to come back, that is."

"I thought getting him out of Mexico was the whole idea."

"Sam tried, but it's no go. Mexico has him for the duration. But the U.S. has made it clear he's an American citizen, and we're watching. Sam talked to him personally and says he's being treated okay." Jake patted my leg. "He did commit a crime, Celia. He has to pay for it. He's just lucky the penalty wasn't worse."

"What about Miguel?"

"I guess he's pretty banged up, but he's going to make it." He got up and turned the TV dial. Marshall Dillon blazed across the screen in pursuit of a gang of outlaws, and I knew the conversation was over.

"Oh, I forgot." Jake spoke up at the commercial. "Sam said Dotty will call you next Sunday night before evening church."

It dawned on me then that I hadn't been to evening church in weeks. As I picked up our half-empty plates and headed toward the kitchen, I decided that would have to change. I rinsed the dishes, set them in the sink, then went back to the dining room and called Jake's mother.

* * *

Aunt Rose had pulled four chairs around a new glass-top patio table and tilted the umbrella to block the worst of the sun. She'd been right about the breeze. It came in spurts, kicking up blades of Uncle Edward's just-mown grass and offering hints of a cooler evening to come.

She served the barbecue chicken cold—"that way it won't draw so many bees," she explained—and set out enough potato salad and deviled eggs for the entire family, ours and Jake's.

"Is Mary Margaret coming?" I asked.

"No, dear." Aunt Rose set a bowl of olives and sweet pickles on the table. "I didn't invite her. Jake, Edward, come sit before the bugs carry it all away." She smiled serenely and handed me a napkin. "Better take two; Edward's chicken can be messy."

We held hands while Uncle Edward said grace. Aunt Rose made small talk all through dinner, but I couldn't shake the feeling that another bomb was about to drop. Jake didn't seem to notice. He finished off half a chicken and three helpings of salad before starting in on the ice cream Aunt Rose served for dessert.

"Ah, Rosebud," Jake sighed and patted his bulging middle. "I sure have missed your cooking."

I knew his comment was meant as a compliment to her and not as a slur to me, but I smacked him just the same. "We've missed you both." I looked from Rose to Uncle Edward. "We've wanted to come out so many times, but with all that's been going on . . ."

Aunt Rose patted my hand. "Now, you just never mind, sweetheart; we understand. Don't we, Edward? I just wish there was more we could do to help." She looked at Uncle Edward out of the corner of her eye, and I knew the fuse had been lit.

Uncle Edward cleared his throat. "Rose and I just wanted you to know we'll help out with the baby in any way we can."

"Edward," Aunt Rose glared across the table, "you know very well that's not all of it." She turned to me. "I know this thing with Libby has been hard, but I do hope you're encouraging her to keep the baby." Jake's face turned ashen, and she hurried on. "You can't let her give it up," she pleaded. "This baby is family, no matter what side of the blanket he's born on." She kept going before anyone could interrupt her. "Edward and I have decided to offer Libby and the baby a home. I know you're going back to work, Cissy, and Jake's busy at the shop. Edward and I have all this room . . . They'd be welcome here, and Libby could learn to be a mother at her own pace."

I didn't know what to say. Jake just sat staring at the napkin in his lap, too deflated to bolt from the table, which is what I knew he wanted to do. The truth was, he wanted Libby to give up the baby for adoption, and I thought I agreed. "She's really too young to be a mother," I'd told Dotty. "Jake and I would wind up raising it, and I don't think either of us is ready to parent an infant again. With my connections, we'll be able to find the perfect home."

But what about Chuck and Grace? The question haunted me, but I pushed it aside. Those were different circumstances, in different times. And this decision seemed so right. Libby had hesitated at the suggestion but reluctantly agreed to "think about it." We hadn't talked about it in several weeks.

"Aunt Rose." I started to explain but knew she'd never understand, so I took another track. "You're so sweet to offer. We're still thinking about what will be best for the baby. And for Libby," I added lamely.

Jake looked at his watch. "I hate to eat and run, but I've got some work to do tonight, and there's church tomorrow morning." He laid his napkin next to his empty ice-cream bowl. "Where's your purse, Celia? I'll get the car."

Aunt Rose looked like she was about to cry. I hugged her hard. "Don't worry. Everything will work out for the best. Haven't you always told me, 'God has a plan'?"

Jake flipped the radio on as soon as we got in the car. So instead of discussing Aunt Rose's invitation, we listened to a commentator talk about racial integration in the military and the troops that had just been sent to Thailand to defend against an attack from Laos.

"I hope," Jake said quietly, "this doesn't mean an escalation of the war."

Chapter
Twenty-seven

The year before, they had padded the dark wooden pews at our church with a burgundy upholstery to match the carpet in the foyer and aisle. The floor underneath the pews was still hardwood, stained dark with age, but clean, of course. The janitors saw to that each Monday afternoon.

All through the doxology and the morning hymn, my eyes kept wandering to the aisle. I could almost see Libby walking down it in a dress of satin and white lace, her hand tucked firmly under her father's arm. Her cheeks would glow with excitement as they moved toward her groom, and Jake would have to concentrate to keep from treading on the train of her gown . . .

The couple next to us handed their little boy three quarters and a dime. When the offering plate passed by, he tried to help himself to more. His mother grabbed his hand, and the change fell to the wooden floor, bouncing noisily in all directions. I couldn't help thinking how if it had been one of hers, Dotty would have soothed the child and explained that the offering was a time to give, not to receive.

It took awhile to regain my composure. My dreams for my daughter had crumbled, and my best friend had moved away at the same time. But this was not the time or place for self-pity. I fished a tissue from my purse and dabbed my eyes.

"What's wrong?" Jake whispered. "Are you sick?"

I whispered, "Just tired," fought back a new barrage of tears and forced myself to listen to the pastor's sermon. As soon as it was over, I grabbed Jake's arm and hustled him out the side door.

"Celia, what's gotten into you?" He was annoyed, but I kept hold of his arm and practically dragged him to the car.

I had seen my share of heartache and trial, but I could think of only a few times when I'd felt completely overwhelmed. That Sunday was one of them.

When we reached home, Jake turned on the ball game and sprawled out on the couch with the Sunday paper. I fixed cold sandwiches for lunch and handed him a bag of chips. "I'm going in to take a nap," I said. He grunted, but didn't look up from the sports page.

Our bed felt like the outfield at a sandlot game. All bumps and hollows, and the bedspread made me itch. I had to cover my face with a pillow to stifle sobs that I just couldn't stop; then my nose would clog and I'd have to sit up and reach for one more tissue to clear it. After half an hour I knew a nap was out of the question. I got up, went into the bathroom and splashed cold water on my face. "Get a grip, girl," I said to the mirror. "This is ridiculous." My face glared back at me, red and ugly and sad to be alive.

An orange-scented breeze drew my attention to the open window. My gardening trowel and gloves sat where I had left them on the patio wall. Determined not to waste the entire day, I changed into long pants and a cotton shirt to protect me from the sun. "I'm going to work in the yard," I said to the back of Jake's head.

"Whoo-ee, Celia, look at this," he yelled, pointing toward the

TV. "The Yankees just took the game, six to one! Mark my words, they're going to win the pennant again this year. No one can touch them."

No one can touch you either, I thought—then, *I'm sorry, that wasn't fair.* Jake had been through just as much as I had this past year—and more. On top of Libby, and our best friends' move, he'd lost his father and taken on responsibilities he hadn't asked for. All the fuss with his ma and Dave and the money missing from the well. I knew he was slipping her a few dollars every week for little things like a new teapot or a magazine. I loved him for that. I loved him for a lot of reasons. *Then why am I so angry with him? He hasn't done a thing to deserve it.*

I tried to talk it out with Dotty when she phoned that afternoon just before five o'clock. "I'm wallowing in self-pity," I complained when Jake was out of hearing range. "You'd think I didn't have a thing to be thankful for, and that's not true. God's seen me through a lot worse than this. What's wrong with me?"

Dotty chuckled. "If you find out, let me know. I'm almost in the same position. We tried another new church today, but it just isn't the same. I try not to complain. Sam's so engrossed with his new job he can't see the light of day. He says it doesn't matter where we worship as long as God's Word is preached. But it does make a difference, Celia. And I have to admit it's hard for me to make new friends."

Jake walked by, tapping his watch and pointing to the telephone. I felt another surge of irritation that turned to guilt when I realized we'd been on the phone for forty minutes. "Time is money," as Papa would have said. And long distance wasn't cheap.

"I've got to go," Dotty blurted. "Mikey just spilled grape juice on David's library book. Don't worry, honey, ten years from now we'll look back on all of this and smile."

"Don't bet on it." I said goodby and hung up the phone.

Jake came out of the kitchen munching another sandwich. "Are you going to evening service?" he asked around a mouthful of bologna. I looked at the clock. If I hurried, I could just make it. "Yes," I decided. If crying couldn't cure what ailed me, maybe the singing and fellowship could. "Do you want to go?"

Jake eyed the TV, then made his decision. "Sure, I'll finish this and change." He stared at my grass-stained knees and muddy shoes. "Fifteen minutes, or we'll be late."

The guest speaker was a missionary from Korea. She told about an adoption agency in Oregon that was rescuing Korean orphans and placing them in homes in the United States. "These babies are unwanted in their country," she said sadly. "Some of them are outcasts because they have Caucasian fathers. In most cases their mothers can't afford to raise them."

She showed slides of sad-faced children with dirty, tear-stained cheeks. Some of them were handicapped, or so undernourished their little ribs stuck out around their bloated bellies. I closed my eyes and thanked God that Libby's baby would have a better start.

A friend of Jake's approached us after the service. "It makes my blood boil," he said. "They put those children out to starve just because they're part white."

"Now dear"—his wife patted his arm and looked apologetically at Jake and me—"at least some of them are coming to a Christian country. They'll be loved and accepted here." They moved off, the husband shaking his head and the wife yoo-hooing to someone across the room.

Jake slipped ten dollars into the special offering envelope, then ushered me out the door into the cool night air. "Want to stop for ice cream?"

I knew he'd asked just out of habit. We used to stop at

Louie's on Sunday nights with Dot and Sam. I shook my head. "I don't think so, not tonight."

He squeezed my hand and opened the passenger door for me, and we drove most of the way home in silence.

"I don't know about you," Jake said as we turned the corner onto Wells Street, "but I'm ready to call it a night."

I agreed. It was only eight o'clock, but the emotions of the day had worn me out. I leaned my head against his shoulder. "I'm so tired I could sleep for a week."

As it turned out, it would be another ten hours before either of us got any sleep.

Chapter
Twenty-eight

I told Stuart later, "I fully expected Miguel's father to be wearing six-shooters and crossed holsters, and smoking a huge cigar."

He patted my hand. "I think you handled the whole thing very well. You've got grit, Celia Freeman." He hesitated, then smiled. "Jake must be proud of you."

I didn't tell him it was Jake who had handled most of it, Jake who first saw the rusty Ford pickup blocking the drive that Sunday night. I didn't mention my fear, or the whispered prayer for strength, or the fact that I obeyed without question when Jake told me, "Stay in the car while I see what this is all about."

There was never a doubt that the couple in the truck were Miguel's parents. Even though I'd never really seen Miguel's face, the man was too old to be him. From behind, all I could see of the woman was dark hair piled in a bun. The rest of her was hidden by the back of the truck seat. The dusty license plate said "Ensenada, Mexico."

Jake parked at the neighbor's curb and got out of the car. "Be careful," I cautioned, laying a hand on his arm.

He squeezed my fingers. "It's all right, Celia, I won't lose my cool."

There wasn't time to tell him that wasn't what I meant.

The truck door opened, and a man in a white shirt, Levis and dusty work boots stepped to the pavement. He snatched a well-worn cowboy hat from his head and stretched out his right hand in a gesture of friendship. Jake hesitated only a moment before holding out his own. They shook hands. The man was so soft-spoken, I could barely hear his words through the open car window.

"Señor Freeman? Mi nombre es Manuel Flores."

"Inglés, Manuel." His wife had climbed out of the truck and was standing by her husband's side. "Speak English, please."

"My apologies. I am Manuel Flores. May I present my wife, Estelle."

I didn't hear Jake's reply. I couldn't take my eyes off Estelle. She had to be at least my age, but her petite figure and caramel-coffee skin made her look at least ten years younger. Her hair was black. Raven black, except for a few gray strands that she made no effort to hide. She wore a colorful, woven-cotton skirt with a hand-embroidered blouse, and I knew without a doubt she had made it herself.

When I tore my eyes away, they were all watching me. I felt my face redden. *Where are your manners, girl?* I hurried over, took Estelle's arm and led Miguel's parents into the house.

Later, when I had slept twelve hours and some of the pressure of the months before had eased, I realized how Mama must have felt when the authorities took Papa off to prison. She had crawled into the closet of her mind and found a peaceful, easy life. The world fell apart around her, and she just refused to take part. I had forgiven her a long time ago, but that night, for the first time, I believe I truly understood.

Estelle and Manuel Flores sat straight and still on the couch across from Jake, who had taken the chair by the window. I picked up a dining-room chair to move it closer to the group. I hadn't taken two steps when Mr. Flores jumped to his feet. He took the chair from me and placed it next to Jake's. Then, with a slight bow, he resumed his seat beside his wife.

Jake studied the carpet for a minute, then looked up and cleared his throat. "How is—your son?"

A flash of pain crossed Estelle's face, then was gone.

"Ah, Miguel, he es better," Manuel answered. Estelle barely said a word the entire visit, except to gently correct her husband's English from time to time.

"It is why we are here. Miguel, he want to come himself, but ..." Mr. Flores shrugged at the obvious.

Jake nodded. Sam had told us the boy was still in a hospital in Mexico City. "I'm sorry. My brother Dave gets carried away. None of us would have wanted this to happen." Jake's voice had hardened, and he made an effort to soften it. "Please tell your son ..."

"Miguel." Estelle's tone was kind, but there was a hint of fire in her eyes.

She's reminding him Miguel's a person, I thought. I would have tried to do the same.

Jake corrected himself. "Please be sure Miguel understands that Celia and I meant him no harm."

They nodded politely, then Mr. Flores reached into his shirt pocket and pulled out two envelopes. "As I say, Miguel, he want to come. He asked us to give you this." His hand shook slightly as he extended the wrinkled envelope toward Jake. "It is for the baby."

I held my breath. Was it money? I couldn't guess what Jake would do. I could tell they didn't mean it as a bribe, but would he understand?

Jake stared at the envelope but made no effort to take it. Mr. Flores laid it gently on the table and drew out another just like it. "And this is from David. When we tell him we are coming, he asks us to give it to you."

This time Jake accepted the envelope, studied the handwriting on the front, then set it next to the other one. "You saw Dave?"

"Sí, señor. We visit him many times. Estelle, she take him soup and tortillas." He shook his head, "Mexican jail very bad. Not much food. And las cucarachas!" He rolled his eyes. Estelle shivered, and her husband continued, "But David, he is well. He say to tell you he is sorry. He says sorry to all of us." Tears spilled down Manuel's brown cheeks. "Por Dios, what are we to do with them? These boys who think they must drink and fight to be a man."

Jake frowned. "I don't understand. My brother nearly killed your . . . Miguel, and you're telling me you visit him in jail? And take him dinner on top of it?"

Manuel Flores looked confused. "Por cierto, amigo. Your David is a son to us. He live with us whenever the boys are in Mexico. He and Miguel, they are like brothers. But we have not come to talk about that. Miguel has done a great disservice to your family. David was defending your Liberty's honor. We respect that. So does Miguel."

Estelle's face had darkened to a reddish hue, and the pain I'd seen before flooded her eyes. She looked at me and spoke, her voice soft and pleading. "Miguel is not a bad boy. He is always polite, and did well in school. He goes to church with us on Sundays. We never thought . . ."

She dropped off lamely and lowered her head in deference to her husband.

"Do not make excuses for him, Estelita. He did wrong and he has been punished. Por Dios, I wish it could turn out another way. But we are a poor family, señor. Miguel is young and cannot afford to support a wife. We will do what we can to help." He gestured to the envelope on the table next to Dave's. "There is money Miguel saved last summer. He said you are to have it. It is not much, but we will find a way to send more. Miguel and David have the fishing boat, and I am working steady right now."

"We don't need your money." Jake's protest went unheeded.

"Estelle, she makes clothes to sell." He fingered the collar on her blouse, where a tiny blue-and-green hummingbird floated above a bouquet of fuchsia blossoms. "Es beautiful, no?" There was no mistaking the love and pride in his eyes.

I squeezed Jake's arm. "Her work is beautiful. I love it. So would Libby."

Estelle's eyes brightened. "You shall each have one, señora. I will send them as soon as we arrive home."

Mr. Flores stood. "We have intruded long enough. Miguel asks to see Liberty and the baby when it comes." Jake looked alarmed and the man rushed on, "I tell him he must ask your permission. When he is well, he will come to apologize in person." He drew his shoulders back and held his head high. "I tell him, he wants to be a man, he will act like one. I cannot force you to receive him, but please keep in mind that he cannot ask God's forgiveness until he has asked for yours."

It was nearly midnight when we saw them to their truck. They were driving straight back to Ensenada. Jake and I held hands and watched the rusty pickup squeak to a stop at the corner of Valley and Wells. Then they were gone, and I realized, as we turned to walk back into the house, that both our palms were damp and we were shaking like aspens in a summer storm.

Chapter
Twenty-nine

Jake and I tried to make some sense out of Manuel and Estelle's visit. We counted the money in the envelope: two hundred dollars in ones and fives. It would pay the hospital bill. "At least the kid is taking some responsibility," Jake conceded.

By the time we finished reading and discussing Dave's letter, it was a quarter to five in the morning and black as pitch outside. "I'm going to bed," Jake said and handed me the letter. "Maybe this will make sense after a couple hours' sleep. I'm so foggy-headed now, I don't know what to believe."

I nodded. "So am I, but I don't think I can sleep yet. I think I'll sit outside awhile."

"Suit yourself. You can sleep all day tomorrow, but I have to be at the shop by nine." He kissed my cheek and shuffled toward the bedroom.

It had been a new-moon night with hardly any stars. Now there was only one visible at all: the morning star twinkling in the eastern sky and already fading with the first flush of dawn. I curled up in a corner of the back porch swing and let the warm, damp darkness wrap around me like the arms of God. *Please, I whispered, show me the truth, show me where to go from here.*

I reached up and flipped the switch on the porch light. A soft yellow glow lit up the area by the door, barely reaching my corner of the swing. But I found that if I turned my back and held Dave's letter up over my head, I could just make out the heavy blue-ink scrawl.

Jake, by now you know I found Miguel. I didn't mean to bust him up so bad. I only wanted to rough him up, show him he couldn't mess with my niece and get away with it. They say I nearly killed him, but I don't remember a thing after the first punch. That scares me almost as bad as this rat hole jail they've got me in. I had popped a few uppers that night. And half a case of beer. I guess you could say I was pretty wasted.

When I told Miguel about Libby, he came unglued. He swore he never forced her, that she came on to him. That's when I slammed him. Took his nose right off his face. Everything after that is just a big red blur. It's been hell since I've been sober. I know it probably doesn't mean much to you, but I swear I'll never touch the stuff again. Not booze or the pills.

Manuel and Estelle came to see me as soon as they knew Miguel wouldn't die. They said they were sorry for what Miguel had done to Libby, and asked for your address. They said, "We forgive you, David." Can you beat that? I nearly kill their son and they forgive me when I didn't even ask them to. They're good people, Jake-O. Please don't blame them for Miguel's mistake.

They probably told you about the fishing boat. It's not very pretty, but the tourists don't seem to mind. It floats—and Miguel knows where to find the big ones, blue-fin tuna, marlin, once in a while a big fat bass. I loaned him the money to buy the boat. That was the money I swiped from the register at the shop. It only took us a couple of weeks to earn it back. I was going to return it at New Year's, but I knew you were torqued out of shape about the cash from the well.

I didn't want to fight with you, so I split. When I did get up the guts to come, we really didn't solve a thing.

So listen up now, big brother. Once and for all: I didn't take Ma's money. Not that I didn't think about it. When I went back to the house to grab my stuff, Pa's letter was face up on the kitchen table. When I read it, I wanted to puke. He never did think I was good enough. I could have stood on my head and danced a jig, but it wouldn't have satisfied him. I wanted to bust something up, so I packed my gear on my bike, got the ax from the garage and found the stupid well.

It wasn't hard. Brian had mowed the grass just a few days before, and I knew it was just beyond the yard behind the wire fence. Brian and John tied me up out there one day when I was five. They didn't come get me till it turned dark, said they forgot all about me, promised they'd whip my hide if I told Ma, and Pa would whip it again for being anywhere near the place. I wasn't a squealer, so I kept quiet, but I knew where to find the well.

I chopped the cover into kindling. But before I could even look for the cash, I heard a car pull up out front. I knew if I didn't split right then, you or Ma would try to stop me. For all I knew, you could have had the cops on me for what happened at the shop. I figured the two hundred would just have to be enough and got my tail out of there. The rest is history, man. Just believe I'm being straight on this one, okay?

Please be nice to the Floreses. They've always treated me like one of their own. When I get out of this hellhole, I'll run the fishing boat for them until Miguel can handle it by himself.

Give Ma my love, and Libby too. I never meant to hurt any of you. I guess I screwed up pretty bad, and I don't blame you for hating my guts.

Dave

I folded the letter and slipped it into the pocket of my dressing gown. An hour earlier neither Jake nor I had known what to believe. But now, as the eastern sky brightened from gray to pink to gold, I realized Dave was telling the truth.

* * *

"It doesn't make sense, Celia. If he didn't take the money, who did?" Jake swallowed the last of his coffee and looked at his watch. "I'm late. Ron must be getting pretty tired of this."

I took his coffee cup and empty toast plate to the sink. "He understands, darling. You told me Ron's had family problems of his own, remember? Besides, you always pay him extra when he has to open."

"It's only what he deserves, Celia."

"I know that; that isn't the point. Oh, never mind. You'd better go." I wrapped my arms around his neck and rested for a minute against the cool cotton fabric of his clean work shirt. By tonight it would be caked with grease and sweat in spite of the overalls he wore to protect it. The auto shop was doing well, and he could have spent his days in the office or working out accounts. Instead, he chose to work right alongside his crew. I admired him for that, and so did they.

He moved aside and reached for his cap on the hanger by the back door. The hanger was an inch-thick piece of pine with four wooden dowels, painted white and decorated with colorful stenciled flowers. Libby had made it for us for Christmas three years ago.

Libby. "What should we tell Libby?" I'd asked Jake for the hundredth time the night before. He'd been adamant. "As little as she has to know. Which is nothing, as far as I'm concerned. If and when Miguel wants to see her, we'll deal with it then."

In a way, I thought he was right. If Libby found out Miguel was in the hospital, and her Uncle Dave in jail, she would no doubt go hysterical. That wouldn't do the baby any good. Yet when I thought about how I would feel if Aunt Rose and Uncle

— *167* —

Edward had kept something like this from me, I had to admit I'd be more upset than if they'd told me in the first place.

Stuart agreed. I called him around nine o'clock that morning to find out when he wanted me to start my job.

"Why not come in next Monday?" He sounded cheerful. "Summer session doesn't start for a week, but I'm not teaching, so we can start this project whenever we want."

I agreed to meet him in the administration office at eight o'clock on Monday morning, and said goodby.

"Wait, Celia," he said. "You sound so tired. Is everything okay?"

Grandma Eva always said, "A tale not told is a tale not spread." But I didn't heed her advice. One hour and half a box of tissues later, I had poured the entire story into Stuart's ear.

"I think he's wrong, Celia. Libby should be told," he said when I confided my uneasiness about keeping all this from my daughter. "She's a tough kid. She can handle it. And better now than if she finds out you've been deceiving her. Still," he paused, "I can't advise you to go against Jake's wishes. You'll have to decide for yourself."

I thanked him and said goodby again, but he stopped me one more time. "I'm here if you need me, Celia. Remember that."

"Thank you, Stuart; that means a lot to me." I hung up feeling better than I had in days.

Chapter Thirty

We drove over to the Freemans' house that evening after Jake got home from work. Ma was doing dishes when we arrived, working at a new stainless-steel sink in the freshly painted kitchen. Brian was out back trimming the hedge, and I could see roses climbing the wire fence he'd mended just a few weeks before.

"Brian's a good boy," Ma said to Jake when he commented about the work. "And such a help." She smiled at Brian through the window, then turned to me. "I'm worried about him, though. This thing with Pam—it's not right. I don't want him to give up his dreams for me."

I couldn't help staring at the just-dyed curls above her wrinkled brow.

"Do you think it looks okay?" She patted the sides of her hair and bent to look at her reflection in a glass cupboard door. "Brian insisted I have it done. I told him he should be buying flowers and candy for his future bride."

"Nonsense, Ma. You deserve it." Jake kissed her cheek and moved toward the back screen door.

"Hey, Bri, come in here, will you? We finally got a letter from Dave."

Brian spun around, and I could have sworn there was a look of terror on his face, like a child caught stealing candy from the dime store. But he held up his hand in greeting, and by the time he set aside the clippers and turned back toward the house, the look was gone. Neither Jake nor Ma seemed to notice a thing, and I decided I must have imagined it.

Ma poured iced tea for us and retrieved soft drinks from the fridge for the men. We sat down around the kitchen table, except for Brian, who chugged his pop and propped himself against the sink. "I'm too dirty to sit," he said with a shrug.

"Suit yourself." Jake opened the letter and read it, modifying some of the content for Ma's benefit. When he was done, Ma's eyes were brimming with tears and Brian's head was down, like he was counting the color patterns on the linoleum.

"My poor boy," Ma sniffed and wiped her eyes with a tissue from her apron pocket. "Well, at least this should prove to you that he didn't steal from his mother."

Jake shook his head, "I don't know, Ma. He's concocted some pretty good stories before. Why should I believe him now?"

Ma's whole body stiffened. She drew herself up tall in the chair, slapped both palms against the table and leaned toward Jake. "Now, you listen to me, Jake Freeman, and use that head of yours for something besides stubbornness. If our Davy had so much money, why would he be scraping a living off a fishing boat down in Mexico when he could be living high on the hog right here in the States? It doesn't make no sense."

"She's right," Brian spoke up. "You got to quit blaming Dave for taking that stupid money."

Jake sank back into the chair. "Well, if he didn't take it, who did?"

Brian shrugged and went back to studying the floor.

Ma Freeman sat back and took a sip of her tea. "Maybe," she spoke softly, "maybe it just don't matter. That money's been nothing but a bushel of trouble. If he could know what's been goin' on, Delbert would come back from the grave and put his boot on a few bottoms." She glared at Jake with what Grandma Eva would have called "the evil eye." I tried to fight the urge to laugh, but when Jake broke into a hearty chuckle, I couldn't help myself. Even Ma smiled.

"Now," she said, "who wants ice cream with their apple pie?"

* * *

The last Friday in June, Jake handed me a check for twenty dollars. "Here," he said, "put this in Libby's birthday card. Anne said she needs new shoes. And maybe she can get a purse besides."

I kissed his cheek. "She'll be thrilled. I'll suggest it in my note. I just wish ..."

"I'm sorry, Celia; we've been over this before. If you go now, you wouldn't be able to go when ... later."

"I know, but eighteen is such a special birthday. And I can tell she's lonesome."

Jake winced. "I can't help that. She's the one ..." He shook his head. "She chose San Francisco, and we just don't have the money to go back and forth."

I changed the subject. "I made her some maternity clothes. We can wrap them and send the package with the card and check. Would you like to see?"

"Not now," he said. "I have some work to do in the garage."

* * *

Libby sounded down when we talked to her on the Fourth of July. "She's pretty depressed," Anne confided when Libby got off the phone and went in to try on her new clothes. "I don't think she's so hot on the idea of giving the baby up. She knows it's for the best, but still ..." Anne paused. "Celia, Chuck and I have been talking. I know you and your boss have been working on finding a home for the baby, but what would you think if we adopted it? We could get married right away and raise it as our own." She hurried on before I could get a word in edgewise. "Oh, don't worry, we'd see to it the baby knew who its mother was. Chuck wouldn't have it any other way. This way the baby could stay in the family, and Libby could see him or her anytime she likes."

I had to reassure myself it was Anne Marie on the phone. The speech was so unlike her. Would she really back down and marry Chuck, just to keep the baby? "Anne, I don't know what to say. Have you talked to Libby about this?"

"No, of course not. We wouldn't do that until we'd spoken to you." She spoke softly, logically again. More like the Anne Marie I knew. "It's not a hasty decision, Celia. Chuck and I have talked it through many times. Just think about it. We've got some time. The baby isn't due until the end of August. Which reminds me. You should plan to come for a couple of weeks. These little ones don't always come when they're expected."

I assured her I'd be there in plenty of time and planned to stay until after the baby came.

Jake looked appalled when I hung up the phone and told him what Anne and Chuck had in mind. "That's the most ridiculous thing I've ever heard. It won't work. Mark my words, it'll just cause more trouble." His face reddened, and his eyes set off their own fireworks. "It's out of the question. You and Haley will just have to keep looking for another home," he said as he walked away, letting the back screen door slam shut on his way out. If Libby had done that, he would have called her back and made her close it quietly.

* * *

"The thought crossed my mind," I told Stuart later, "but I didn't think it was very good timing."

Stuart laughed. "Wise choice. I don't think he would have appreciated the humor."

Stuart's office was an eight-by-ten-foot space filled with a brown leather sofa, an enormous desk, file cabinets and a double-wide bookshelf that held everything from Jung to Chaucer to the *Encyclopedia Britannica*. The shelves also supported a battery radio, several high-school basketball trophies and a nine-inch black-and-white television set. There was little room for movement in the crowded space, and I sat forward on the sofa to reach the file folder he handed across the desk.

He gripped my hand and squeezed. "Don't worry, it will all work out. Take a look at this."

I knew the file contained another of the case histories we were compiling for our research, but when I scanned the first page, I couldn't help gasping.

"Stuart, this is Grace," I said, flustered. "I mean Florence. I thought you wanted me to interview her."

He smiled. "I did at first, but you've been so preoccupied. I thought, under the circumstances, maybe I could be a more objective listener." He cleared his throat. "It looks as if she had a pretty good childhood in spite of the deception involved." He motioned to the folder. "Take it home and read it. See if you think my evaluation is fair."

He cleared his throat again. "By the way, your brother wouldn't talk to me. He was rude, actually. Do you think you could get somewhere with him? His case would really give this thing some balance, but I don't want any lawsuits."

I winced. "Chuck is still sensitive about the whole thing. Anne says he seldom talks about the past, and then only in a negative way."

I thought about the few things Chuck had told me about his relationship with the DuVals. He had been already five when they adopted him. Too old to be fooled by their lies, and too young to understand their motives. Even after all these years, he was convinced they had taken him only because Sister Veronica had insisted he and the baby be kept together. If he was right, who could blame him for resenting them?

"He keeps in touch with Flo," Stuart said. "She said she got a letter from him just the other day. Maybe we should go through her."

I shook my head slowly. "I don't know, Stuart. Let me try. But if he still balks, I'd rather not force the issue, okay?" I wondered if he would think I'd overstepped my bounds. After all, I was just an assistant. I was used to following orders, but I felt this case was a little different.

I shouldn't have worried.

"Fair enough." He leaned his chair back toward the window and clasped both hands behind his head. "So, when do you leave for San Francisco?"

"Not until the end of August. But I figure I'll need at least three weeks. Even if the baby's on time and we have a home for it right away, Libby will need me when she gets out of the hospital."

He nodded. "Take all the time you need. I'm only teaching one class in the fall, and we have a full eighteen months to finish this project."

He got up and came around the desk. "That means we can spend some time finding the perfect parents for Libby's child." He pulled me to my feet and handed me my bag from the corner of the desk. "Let's go talk to Social Services. I made an appointment for eleven." He hooked his arm through mine and led me out the door.

Chapter
Thirty-one

In August 1962, the temperature stayed at ninety-nine degrees for two solid weeks, Marilyn Monroe died from an overdose of sleeping pills, and Liberty Jane Freeman was in a perpetual state of hysteria.

We called the first Sunday of the month to tell her we had found a home for the baby. She started sobbing, and I couldn't understand a word she said until she shouted, "Quit trying to run my life." When I put the receiver back to my ear, I was listening to dead air.

I redialed. Chuck answered on the first ring, but he wouldn't talk to me either. "You'll have to wait until Anne gets her calmed down," he said coldly. "We'll call you back."

"What on earth?" I complained to Jake. "I thought she'd be happy we'd finally made some progress."

The truth was, Stuart and I had gotten nowhere with the Social Services people. Oh, they had hundreds of families interested in adopting an infant, but the process was expensive and slow. Jake had listened only halfheartedly to my complaints about interviews and paperwork, but as time grew short, he finally made a suggestion. "Why don't you call that agency in Oregon, the one that missionary went on about?"

I got the number and called the next day from Stuart's office. The staff member I talked to was kind. She explained that they dealt only with foreign adoption, but gave me the numbers of several private agencies to try. My next call produced an interview.

"We have the perfect couple," the agency director said. "They're college graduates with a good income and impeccable backgrounds, and they meet all the physical requirements. If we can get the paperwork completed soon, they can take the baby as soon as it's ready to leave the hospital."

I wondered once again if we were doing the right thing, but Stuart reassured me. "You said yourself Libby's too young to be a mother. You'd wind up raising the baby yourself, and you know Jake won't agree to that."

He was right, and yet I couldn't help but think of Chuck and the trauma he'd been through. Even Florence had to admit it was quite a shock to find out she hadn't been born to the parents who had raised her. *But their situation was different,* I assured myself. Most adoptive parents were more open with their children, and in cases like Libby's, a two-parent family was usually better for the baby.

"Maybe we should reconsider Chuck and Anne Marie's offer," I said aloud.

Jake looked at me like I'd grown two heads. "No."

I had wrestled with the decision and prayed until I was blue in the face, and adoption still seemed to be the best answer for everyone, including the baby. Why, then, was Libby balking now when she had already agreed to give it up?

I whispered a prayer for wisdom and sat down on a dining-room chair to wait for Anne's call.

The phone rang ten minutes later. "Celia." Anne was calm but short of breath. "Libby's pretty shook up. I think I'll run her in to the office and have Dr. Williams give her something."

She hesitated, then added, "Maybe you should come a few weeks early. She's been homesick, and I know she's scared."

I didn't have to think about my answer. "I'll be there tomorrow afternoon."

"Be where?" Jake sat hunched into the sofa cushions, looking for all the world like a sulking child.

"In San Francisco. Libby needs me, Jake." I spoke softly but felt a new resolve, as if this was the first right decision I had made in months. "Our daughter needs me," I repeated, "and I'm going to her."

"Thank the Lord, he didn't say 'I need you too,' " I told Stuart over the phone the next morning. "I think I would have smacked him."

I could hear his quiet chuckle on the other end of the line. "Well, don't worry. I'll handle things on this end. We won't make any commitments until Libby's ready."

I hung up, grateful for his understanding.

*　*　*

Jake helped me check my bags and walked me through the busy train station. We sat in silence, listening to the babble around us. Then the sound system rattled, and a bland voice announced, "Train number 16 from Los Angeles to San Francisco will begin boarding in five minutes on track 5."

"That's you." Jake stood, and I stood with him. "Don't worry, babe, everything will turn out fine." He wrapped me in a hug, and I thought for a minute he might not let me go. He kissed me fiercely, then pulled away. "Be careful now. And call me when you get there."

He handed me the carry-on bag I'd packed with an apple and the latest *Good Housekeeping* magazine. "You'd better go." He pushed me gently toward the line of passengers already snaking toward the turnstile. "Give my love to Libby and Anne Marie."

"I will. I love you, darling." I mouthed the words, but he had already turned away.

* * *

The station in San Francisco was crowded, but I spied Chuck right away. He's so handsome, I thought. A blond, blue-eyed Adonis, with Mama's eyes and Papa's crooked smile. He saw me then. He pressed forward through the crowd until he reached my side and wrapped me in an awkward hug. "Hi, sis. How was your trip?" Long, smoky, hot and crowded. "Fine," I lied, then added, "It's good to see you. Where are Libby and Anne Marie?"

His mouth twitched, and I realized that what I had taken for a smile was really the thin purplish scar that ran from his chin halfway up his right cheek.

"They're at home," he said. "The doctor put Libby to bed for a few days, but Anne thinks she should stick close to home until the baby comes." He winced when he said Anne's name, and I knew he carried other scars besides the ones on his face. "We try not to leave Libby alone," he went on as he guided me to the baggage claim area. "Having you here will make it easier."

On the way to Anne Marie's, we talked about the weather and his job—anything but Libby and our plans for the baby. Traffic was heavy, and our conversation slowed as Chuck guided his Corvette up and down winding hills and over cable-car tracks until he reached the bay. He pulled into a parking lot overlooking the ocean and turned off the engine. "How about a look at San Francisco?" he said, pushing himself out of the car before I could respond.

I joined him at a low cement wall overlooking the water, where tourists scanned the ocean and hills with the help of large, powerful scopes. He pointed out a few of the sights: Alcatraz Island, the famous Golden Gate Bridge and Fisherman's Wharf. I could just make out a sign that read "Arturo's Steak

Chapter Thirty-one

House."

"That will be my place someday," Chuck said matter-of-fact-ly. "Right now I just run the kitchen."

I laid my hand against his arm. "I'm proud of you. We all are. You've made a good life for yourself."

He shrugged. "Not good enough for Anne Marie."

"Charles Summers! Anne Marie adores you. I thought—I mean, she said you two had finally decided to get married."

"That was when she thought we had a chance to adopt the baby. Now she's having second thoughts. Again." The pain on his face was rapidly replaced with the sober, blank expression I had seen since we'd left the station.

I closed my eyes. The wind whipped off the ocean, and I shivered in spite of the afternoon sunshine. What could I say? If it was wrong for Anne Marie to marry someone who didn't share her faith, wouldn't it be worse to marry him so they could raise someone else's child?

Once again my brother seemed to read my thoughts. "It's complicated, Cissy." He stared down into the cold white waves that smacked the sea wall. I thought he would let it go at that, and I was trying to think of the right thing to say when he turned to face me. "I just want you to know that it's not your fault. It wouldn't have worked, and Anne and I both know that. Rescuing a baby is no foundation for marriage." He turned back to the sea. Rescuing a baby. Did our baby need rescuing?

"We're breaking it off. As soon as the baby is born and Libby doesn't need us anymore. It'll be hard living in the same town with Anne Marie, but . . ." He let the sentence drop.

The wind stung my eyes, and I turned my back on the ocean. Chuck turned with me, and we stood side by side looking out over the parking lot watching tourists, mostly couples, come and go. Some laughing and joking, others unsmiling and silent. *What could be so wrong,* I wondered, that they have nothing to say to each other?

"I believe in God," Chuck said, and I remembered his habit of speaking up, right out of the blue, like there had never been a break in the conversation. "I go to church with her on Sundays. Heck, I've lived like a monk for the last seven years. But it's not enough for her. No matter what I do, it's never enough."

All of my brother's carefully masked emotions were now running rampant across his face. I saw frustration and anger and, most of all, genuine grief.

"You really love her."

"More than life," he said.

"Well, that's how God loves you, Chuck. More than life. That's why Jesus died. And your pain is nothing compared to the grief he feels when you refuse him." The words were out before I could even think what I was saying.

He stared at me wide-eyed, as if I'd slapped him in the face, then took my arm and led me back to the car.

Chapter
Thirty-two

Libby refused to even look at the adoption papers. She was angry one minute and terrified the next, her weeping so intense that we all feared for her and the baby's safety.

Jake called several times toward the end of the month to tell us that Sam had done a background check on the prospective parents and they had come out clean. "I knew you'd want to be sure they were solid," he said. "But Libby needs to snap out of it and make a decision. The agency keeps calling, and I don't know what to tell them." He sounded impatient. "It's not fair to keep these people dangling. They have a right to know."

I knew he was right, but his tone made me mad. "What would you like me to do, Jake, forge her signature? Libby is in no condition to make the decision right now."

"Then make it for her and get her to sign." His voice dropped, and I could hear the sadness behind his words. "We need to get this over with, so we can get back to a normal life."

* * *

Libby came out of her room at four in the afternoon on the last day in August. She had washed her hair and dabbed a little makeup on her face. "Hi, Mom," she said. Her blue-shadowed eyes held the first spark of interest I'd seen in her since the day

I arrived.

She hugged me and balanced the best she could on a kitchen chair. Her belly bulged with the baby's weight, and her ankles were so swollen I was amazed she could even walk. "How do you feel?" I probed gently. The last thing I wanted was to start the tears again.

"Terrible," she grinned. "I hope this little moose decides to make an appearance soon." She accepted the glass of orange juice I handed her. "Where's Aunt Anne?"

"Sleeping. She worked the night shift, but she said to wake her if you needed anything. Are you sure you're okay?"

Libby nodded. "When she wakes up and Uncle Chuck gets here, I want to call Daddy on the phone. I . . . I've made a decision about the baby, and I want you all to hear it."

I started to ask, but the look on her face told me to let it go. It was the same look Mama had when she'd issued a warning and expected to be obeyed. The same determined look I'd seen, more times than I could count, in Mary Margaret's eyes.

Libby spent the next two hours on the sofa with her feet propped up, calmly writing a letter to Rachel. I felt as nervous as Anne Boleyn waiting for the guillotine to fall. I couldn't sit still; by six o'clock, I had cooked dinner, washed and hulled strawberries for our dessert and cleaned everything in sight.

Anne got up just as Chuck arrived. Libby greeted them both with smiles and hugs.

"I think Libby has something to tell us," I said, when we were all assembled in the living room.

Libby nodded, heaved herself off the sofa and waddled to the phone. "I want Daddy to hear this," she said and dialed our number in San Gabriel.

"Daddy?" she said into the mouthpiece. "Daddy, I have something to say to you and Mom and everyone, okay?"

Jake must have responded, because she nodded again, then

took a deep breath and continued, "I want you all to know I love you and how sorry I am for the trouble I've caused. I know I don't deserve your trust or your respect," her voice broke. "I . . . I don't deserve this baby either, but," she hurried on, "I have it, and I'm going to keep it." Anne Marie gasped, and Chuck looked down at his feet with an odd smile on his face. I could only stare at my daughter and wonder what was coming next.

"Please, Daddy, don't say anything. Let me finish, okay?" Tears were coursing down her cheeks again, but I knew she was in control. And it was obvious that now she was speaking directly to Jake. "I made a mistake. Probably the biggest one of my life. I don't love Miguel—not enough to marry him—but I love his child. I know you want me to give it away, and maybe that would work out best for you, but not for me, and not for my baby either. It's part of me, Daddy, just like I'm part of you and Mom."

She sank down on the carpet, with her back propped up against the wall. "I know I can't do it alone. I need your help, just for a little while. Yours and Mom's. This is right, Daddy, I know it is. Please trust me just one more time."

My own eyes blurred and overflowed. I pried the receiver from my daughter's hand, told Jake I'd call him right back and knelt beside her. Even as I rubbed Libby's icy fingers and smoothed back her damp hair, I knew a peace I had thought I'd never have again.

I had no idea what the future would bring, except that Libby was right: for better or worse, this baby would stay with the family.

* * *

The airport was a madhouse. Vacationing families slumped in hard-backed seats, the adults trying to ignore their squabbling offspring as they waited for a flight back home. Incoming college students pushed through the double doors, greeted their friends and propelled themselves down the escalators.

I stood on tiptoe trying to get a glimpse of the door. Jake's plane had touched down ten minutes ago.

It was September 3, the day after my fortieth birthday. I had called him from the hospital at one a.m. to let him know his grandson had been born, all eight pounds, ten ounces of him. "A boy, huh?" His voice was groggy with sleep. "Too bad he missed your birthday by an hour. How's Libby?"

"She's okay now, but she had a rough time. The baby was big." My voice cracked, and I took a moment to compose myself. "The baby is fine. The doctor said he's healthy, and you should see all the hair! He's adorable, darling. Just wait until you see him."

"All babies are adorable, Celia, even when they're ugly as sin." He had gone quiet then, and I thought for one horrible minute that he would refuse to come. But he cleared his throat and said, "There's a flight that lands at two this afternoon. I'll see you then."

The crowd thinned, and I finally had a decent view of the passengers hurrying through the double doors.

A teenage girl, wearing enough makeup to paint a house, welcomed her boyfriend with a kiss better suited for the bedroom. They clung to each other until they reached the top of the escalator, then jumped onto the moving stairway and went back into a clinch.

"Jealous?"

I whirled around. Jake's eyes were bright with mischief as he swept me into his arms, glued his lips to mine and lowered me backward almost to the floor.

A couple of grinning students started to clap, and Jake faked a deep bow in their direction.

I felt my face heat up and grabbed his arm. "Good grief," I whispered, "let's get out of here."

"As you wish, madam." He ushered me toward the escalator. "What's the matter, aren't you glad to see me?"

"Of course I am." I held onto the railing and gazed up at him. His face was thinner than a month ago, with tiny lines I'd never seen before around his eyes and mouth, and his hair was peppered with a lot more gray. "I missed you, darling. You'll never know how much."

He stepped off the escalator behind me and nodded toward the outer doors. "Everything I have's in here." He held up a single carry-on bag.

I handed him the keys. He stowed his bag in the trunk of Anne Marie's Volkswagen and slid behind the wheel. But instead of turning the ignition, he reached into his pocket and pulled out a small red box. "Happy birthday, babe. Sorry it isn't wrapped; I didn't have time."

The hinges on the box were stiff, but I finally popped it open. "Oh, Jake, it's beautiful!" I lifted the silver locket from the box and held it to my neck. "Here, help me put it on."

"Aren't you going to look inside?"

The clasp was small and harder to open than the box, but what I found inside made it worth the trouble. "It's Libby, when she was a baby." I turned and looked at him. "Wherever did you find this?"

He grinned. "In that old album you keep in the linen closet. I had the dickens of a time trying to cut it to fit." He pointed to the blank side of the heart-shaped frame. "There's room for another one. I thought, maybe the baby . . ."

I touched his cheek and kissed him, a kiss the couple in the airport would have never understood. "It's perfect, darling. Thank you."

He smiled and started the car.

Chapter
Thirty-three

For someone who was going to disappear right after the baby was born, Chuck was rarely out of sight. He haunted the hospital nursery, pacing back and forth from Libby's room and hounding the nurses to let him hold the baby.

Anne finally lost her patience. "Charles Summers, if you don't sit down, they're going to throw you out of here, and there won't be a thing I can do about it." Then she softened her voice. "Why don't you go home and get some sleep? Visiting hours are at two and eight. You can hold the baby when we get him home."

He obeyed, but when Jake and I got to the hospital at eight that night, Chuck was again in Libby's room. He greeted us, then stepped aside so Jake could see his daughter.

"Hi, sugar." Jake kissed her cheek and handed her the single yellow rose he'd picked out in the gift shop.

"Hi, Daddy. Thanks," she said weakly. "Have you seen him yet?"

"Now who would that be?" Jake teased.

"Jesse Michael Freeman," she said proudly. "I named him Jesse for Great-grandma Freeman, and Michael for Miguel. I want him to know his heritage. All of it."

Jake flinched but had the grace to smile. "That's a beautiful name, sweetheart. When can I see him?"

Chuck was already at the door. "I'll take you. There's too many of us in here anyway." He winked at the nurse who had just poked her head into the room.

She wrinkled her nose at him and announced, "Ten minutes, then it's lights out."

"Hey, I just got here," Jake started to argue, but Libby interrupted him.

"It's okay, Daddy. I'm kind of tired. Will you come back tomorrow?"

Jake looked at her with such tenderness, I had to turn my head. "I'll be here, honey," he said softly. "Wild horses couldn't keep me away." He glared at the nurse, who looked from him to Chuck, then threw up her hands in defeat and left the room.

We walked down to the nursery, where a soft fluorescent light glowed behind a plate-glass window. Jesse was in the third bassinet from the left, swaddled from neck to toes in a white blanket. The attendant wheeled him closer so Jake could get a better view.

I held my breath. Jesse's face was a creamy caramel color, defined by narrow black brows and long dark lashes. Tufts of raven-colored hair stuck out at random from beneath the white knit cap. While we watched, he opened his eyes, screwed his mouth into a tiny bow, then relaxed and settled back to sleep.

"Will you look at that!" Jake crowed. "He smiled at me."

I didn't have the heart to tell him little Jesse probably just needed to burp.

"He looks like Pa."

"Maybe," Chuck countered. "I think he looks like Uncle Ed."

I left them there, noses pressed against the nursery window, and went to find Anne Marie.

* * *

We were back the next day at a quarter to two. After a brief stop at the nursery, we hurried on to Libby's room. Jake sat in a padded wooden chair next to the window. The cubicle next to Libby's was empty, so I borrowed a chair from there. Chuck and Anne Marie were standing at the foot of the bed holding hands. Anne was off-duty, and if she was nervous about breaking the "two visitors at a time" rule, she didn't show it.

Libby shifted gingerly beneath the covers. She had fed the baby just before we got there, and I could tell she was getting tired. "We'd better go, dear," I kissed her forehead and started to stand.

"Not yet, Mama, please." She plucked at a piece of lint on the cotton spread. "I wanted to ask if anyone's heard from Uncle Dave."

Chuck coughed and ducked his head. Anne Marie turned away. Libby caught the look that flashed between Jake and me.

"You have, haven't you? And something's wrong. Is it Miguel?" Her face was flush, her wide eyes already brimming with tears.

"Libby, please don't get upset." I grabbed her hand, "It's okay."

Jake took a deep breath, pushed out of his chair and came to stand beside the bed. "All right. Would everyone please excuse us? I'd like to talk to Libby alone."

My mouth went dry. "Jake, are you sure?"

"Don't worry, Celia. Chuck, will you take your sister and Anne for something to drink?"

"This way, ladies." Chuck gave a mock bow and held the door. But instead of escorting us down to the first-floor coffee shop, he put some change in the pop machine, handed us each a bottle of Coke and stood guard with his back against the door of Libby's room.

"Don't worry." Anne Marie took my hand. "Libby is stronger

than you think, and she's more stable now that the baby's been born. I'm sure Jake will handle it."

A few minutes later a nurse came by with a stethoscope in one hand and a thermometer in the other. She took one look at Chuck, guarding the door like a White House sentry, turned around and hustled toward the nurses' station.

Jake came out of Libby's room at a quarter to three. "She's fine," he said to everyone in general. He turned to me. "She wants to see you, Celia; then I think she wants to sleep awhile."

The head nurse was charging down the hall in our direction. I ducked through the door just before she reached the room.

Libby's eyes were red, but she was calm. "If Miguel does come, I want to see him, Mom." She said it softly, but I heard her unspoken edict: *Is that clear?*

* * *

Jake stayed two days, then went back to the shop. He returned the next Saturday afternoon with the car and insisted we make the ten-hour return trip the very next day.

It was still ninety degrees outside, and I was grateful for the ocean breeze blowing through the open car windows. Libby shifted uncomfortably in the back seat, and we had to make several stops for her to stand and stretch. The baby slept contentedly, waking only twice to be changed and fed.

It was dark when we arrived home. I carried the baby into the living room, handed him to Libby and went over to admire a huge bouquet of flowers on the dining-room table. The card read "Happy Fortieth! Love, Dot and Sam." Next to the flowers was a stack of cards and a pink ceramic shoe brimming with violets and baby's breath. "Libby," I called, "come see what Dotty and Sam sent you."

"Oh, Daddy, it's beautiful!"

I turned and saw Libby standing in the doorway to her room. Jake stood behind her, thumbs hooked in the pockets of his jeans, his face wreathed in a boyish grin.

I went to stand beside them. "What is it, Libby? Let me see."

She moved aside. Next to the far wall was a natural-wood crib decorated with a pink and blue lamb decal. A blue and white bumper pad lined the wooden bars, and a colorful cotton quilt was folded over the end.

"Rosebud made the liner and the quilt," Jake said. "I found the crib down at Kid's Palace. There's some other stuff over there. I didn't know where to put it all." In the corner by the dresser was a diaper bag and a pile of assorted baby supplies. Mary Margaret had sent most of it, with a note that read "Good luck, Baby. I'll see you soon."

Aunt Rose and Uncle Edward came on Monday with a stack of diapers and a changing table. Brian and John brought their mother over after work. Ma Freeman handed Libby three hand-made receiving blankets, kissed her cheek, then went over to steal the baby from Aunt Rose.

By the time they all went home at nine o'clock, Libby was exhausted. Little Jesse, blanketed and gowned with gifts from his doting relatives, slept peacefully in the crib.

"I think we should all make it an early night." Jake yawned and pushed out of his recliner.

I was about to join him when Libby spoke up. "What's this stack of mail on the dining-room table?"

Jake looked at the pile of cards and letters. "Sorry. Most of those came on Friday before I left to pick you up. There's been so much going on, I forgot about it."

Libby sifted through the pile and handed me a birthday card from Flo and Jerry, one from Stuart and a note from the Fergusons down the street inviting us to dinner on the tenth.

I showed the Fergusons' note to Jake. "Can you imagine? They've never had the time of day for us—or anyone else on the block, for that matter."

"Well, it doesn't take a rocket scientist, Celia. We're in the same boat they were in several years ago. Except we didn't run from our trouble."

"Jake, hush!" I glanced at Libby, but she was absorbed in the stack of cards and notes addressed to her. "Who are they from, honey?"

Her eyes glowed as she flipped through the envelopes. "Carol, Rachel, Aunt Sara and Uncle Steve. . . ." Her voice faltered as she examined a letter in an air-mail envelope. I stepped forward to see better, and she jerked it back, but not before I saw the return address.

"It's probably from Uncle Dave."

But her hands were shaking. I knew, sure as I was standing there, that it was a letter from Miguel.

Chapter
Thirty-four

I found that letter just a year ago, in a box of things Libby had left behind:

Dear Libby,

I am sorry for what has happened. I don't have much to offer you or our baby, but if you want to get married we can live here with my family. David is running the charter boat until I am well enough to take over. I will send money when I can. Please write and tell me if we have a girl or a boy, and tell me what you want to do.

Miguel

I don't know what she told him. I didn't even read the other letters. I do remember that the next morning Libby handed her father a money order for twenty-five dollars. "Here, Daddy. I know it's not enough, but as soon as I can, I'll get a job."

Jake almost didn't take it. He turned away, then thought better of it and reached out his hand. "I'll open an account. You and Jesse will need it later."

* * *

I went back to work the first week in October. I still missed the crisp morning air and golden leaves that marked the change from summer to fall where I grew up back in Pike. Here in

California we were still sweltering in ninety-degree heat. Libby kept the baby in a diaper and undershirt most of the time.

Other parts of the country—and the world for that matter— were sweltering too, and not just from the weather. Every time we turned on the news, there was another outbreak of violence between Negroes and whites.

"Why are they acting like that, Mother? Those people have a right to go to whatever school they want."

"The segregationists don't think so," her father said dryly. "They think the Bill of Rights is just for them."

"Well," I said, "if you ask me, Kennedy ought to put an end to this nonsense once and for all."

"He has to be careful, Celia. Those guys with the baseball bats pay his salary."

"So do the black students, Jake."

"Hey, don't get on me. I'm not involved with this."

* * *

"I don't know why everything I say has to escalate into an argument," I told Stuart the next day at work. "Jake seems fine with Libby and the baby. All of a sudden I'm the bad guy."

Stuart patted my hand sympathetically, then turned to a stack of files on the edge of the desk. "Here, go through these, will you? We need to decide which of these families to inter- view. Some of them have already turned us down once. Your brother included."

I flushed. "I am sorry, Stuart. I told you I didn't think he'd cooperate. He's having a tough time right now."

"Still carrying the torch for Anne Marie?"

I nodded. "He really loves her. And she loves him, I know it. But she won't—can't—compromise her beliefs."

Stuart frowned. "I don't see how it's a compromise. You said Chuck believes in God. What more does she want?"

I tried to explain Anne's feelings once again, but it was like blowing into the wind.

Frustrated, I decided I'd have better luck if I just hunkered down to the files in front of me. But concentration was practically impossible. The office was stuffy in spite of the open window. Outside, palm fronds hung motionless as heat waves bounced off the pavement into the smoggy air.

I finally laid a stack of letters on Stuart's desk and told him I was leaving early. "I can't concentrate in this heat, and the smog is getting worse. I'd better go before the bus tires melt."

He mopped his forehead with an already soggy handkerchief. "I can't let you take the bus. If you wait up a minute, I'll drive you."

He dropped me off at the curb, but the minute I got in the house, I wanted to flag him down and go back to the office. The baby was fussing, and Libby was a wreck. "I don't know what to do," she sobbed. "I've fed him, changed him and given him a bath. He wants to be held, but it's so hot he breaks out in a rash."

Jake rushed in at five-thirty and snapped on the TV. "Woo-ee, looks like the Yankees are gonna take the series again. Celia, can't you quiet the baby? I'm trying to listen to the game."

"I'd be happy to explain that to him," I hollered from the kitchen, "but by the time he understands, your dinner will be burnt to a crisp."

"Well, you don't have to snap at me! Doggone it, Roger Maris just hit a homer and I missed it!"

"Mother, Daddy, please, you're scaring the baby," Libby shouted over Jesse's screams.

I took a deep breath. "Libby, why don't you take Jesse out on the patio? Maybe the fresh air will quiet him down."

The kitchen was beginning to smell like burnt cheese. As I grabbed a potholder and yanked the casserole from the oven, I had the most awful impulse to dump the entire mess into the garbage and let them fend for themselves. Instead I set the dish in its chrome-handled cradle, slapped a loaf of bread and a half-gallon of milk on the kitchen table, and called, "Dinner's ready!"

"In a minute," Jake said. "One more inning and the series is ours."

Libby marched through the door with her nose in the air and a sleeping Jesse in her arms. "I'm not hungry," she huffed. "We'll be in our room."

Jake strolled into the kitchen after the last inning, acting for all the world as if he'd batted in the winning run himself. "We did it." He grinned and plopped into his chair. "Hey, aren't you going to eat? Where's Libby?"

"I'm too hot to eat," I said. "I'm going to take a shower."

* * *

I had just fallen asleep on the couch when the phone rang.

"Celia, this is Dotty. Have you guys heard the news?"

"No. I mean, Jake was watching the game, then we turned the TV off. What's going on?"

"It looks like the Russians have set up launching sites for nuclear missiles in Cuba. They could strike the United States in a minute. The president sent in the Marines and set up a naval blockade. Then he issued an ultimatum for the missiles to be destroyed or else we'll attack.

"It's awful, Celia. Washington is the first place they'll hit if they use those things. We had to pack bags with food and water, just in case we have to head for a shelter. The grocery stores back here are already sold out of canned goods."

I couldn't help thinking she was overreacting, but when we said goodby, I hung up and turned on the news. Jake came in from the garage just as one of the local newscasters advised people not to panic. "Just be prepared. And remember, this station will broadcast emergency instructions if the need arises."

I grabbed my purse. "There's plenty of canned meat and vegetables," I told Jake, "but we'd better stock up on formula and bottled water. Would you please explain this to Libby? And try not to scare her."

He looked disgruntled, but when I got back home I noticed he had put new batteries in all the flashlights and filled several Thermoses with water.

"Thank God we don't have any loved ones in the service right now," I said as we were crawling into bed.

"I know, but don't forget Vietnam. It doesn't look good in that neck of the woods either. Mark my words, Celia, if Kennedy doesn't do something fast, we're in for another world war."

I shuddered. "All this violence. What kind of a world is this for little Jesse to grow up in? Stuart says if all this internal fighting doesn't stop, we'll destroy the nation ourselves. The commies won't have to do a thing."

"The wise man has spoken," Jake said sarcastically. He rolled over and pecked my cheek just below the ear. "Good night. I'm going to get some shuteye before the baby sounds reveille."

He was snoring when Jesse woke up at one a.m. I slipped into my robe and joined Libby in the kitchen. I took a bottle out of the refrigerator, set it in a saucepan of water and turned the burner on low.

Libby looked as drained as I felt. "I'll change him," I volunteered. "Why don't you get something to eat?"

She didn't argue. "I'm so tired," she groaned. "Being a mother is hard." I didn't even try to hide my smile.

Chapter
Thirty-five

I set the dining-room table with Aunt Rose's silver and Mama's good flowered-china plates.

"Your mama would be so pleased to see you using these," Aunt Rose commented as she placed a dish of fresh-cut mums in the center of the table.

I sighed. "She and Papa would have loved to see the baby, too."

"Well, now," she smiled, "the Bible doesn't say, but you never know. Maybe they can."

I hugged her hard and went to get the pilgrim candles I'd bought the week before. When I came back into the room, Aunt Rose was standing at the window, looking out at something only she could see. She didn't turn, and I studied her profile for a moment, suddenly aware of how thin she'd become. The skin on her neck and face looked twice as wrinkled as when I'd seen her last, and her arms were nothing but skin and bones. *She's only sixty,* I thought, alarmed. *But she looks eighty-five.*

She turned then, and smiled. The same reassuring smile that had brightened my life for almost twenty-seven years. *Aunt Rose is fine,* I told myself. Still, I made up my mind to ask Uncle Edward about it later.

"I'm so glad you agreed to come here for Thanksgiving," I said. "It made it so much easier for Libby and the baby. Jake's mother too."

"We're glad to do it, dear, but it's so much work for you."

"Who is working too hard?" Ma Freeman poked her head into the kitchen. "Rose, you're looking lovely, as usual. Where do you want the sweet potatoes, Celia? Brian's bringing in the pies."

I popped the potatoes into the oven to keep them warm and studied the pies as Brian took them out of a large cardboard box and lined them up on the kitchen counter. "Mother Freeman, you brought so much!"

"Not so much. Oh, your table looks lovely. Where is my Jake? And Libby and the baby? My neighbor made Jesse the cutest sweater."

She fluttered toward the bedroom, where Libby and Mary Margaret had just taken little Jesse to diaper him. Mary Margaret had claimed the baby as soon as she walked in the door, refusing to relinquish him to anyone else, including her mother.

"You get to see him all the time" was her assessment of the situation. It was hard to argue with, but I had a feeling she might have some trouble convincing Jake's Ma.

The men had congregated around the television, but they came quickly enough when I called them to dinner.

Uncle Edward blessed the food: "Dear heavenly Father, we are truly thankful for your bountiful provisions. We are thankful for this home, our health and family. We thank you for little Jesse and what he means to all of us. And," he paused, "we thank you that our country is still free. Amen."

"Amen." The chorus echoed around the table.

"Boy, I have to hand it to Kennedy," Jake said. "He didn't mess around. Jumped in there and cleaned up that entire mess in thirteen days."

Uncle Edward nodded. "I didn't vote for him, but I'll admit

he's proved to be good for the country. In this case, anyway."

"Kennedy, shmennedy," Ma chimed in, "pass the mashed potatoes, Jake, the gravy's getting cold."

* * *

By December the weather finally cooled enough to wear a sweater in the evening. The baby was sleeping through most nights. Libby had recovered her strength and was growing restless.

"Why don't you go to the social at church on Christmas Eve?" I asked her. "Carol's mother said Carol would be there."

"Well, she won't," Libby said, looking up from the game show she was watching on TV. "Carol and Ritche eloped last Saturday night. They borrowed his father's truck and drove to Reno."

"Her poor mother!"

Libby shrugged. "It happens all the time. Anyway, it's about time they got married."

Now what does that mean? I thought. But I didn't have the nerve to ask. "What about the church party, Libby? You really should get out more. You know we'd be happy to watch little Jesse."

She sighed and snapped off the television. "You don't understand, Mom. It's not that easy. I don't have any friends there anymore." I started to argue, but she interrupted. "Mom, I've been thinking. I want to go back to school. I can't let you and Daddy support me all my life, and I can't get a decent job without a high-school diploma."

I nodded. "I think that's a good idea, hon. Maybe you can pick up some high-school credits at PCC."

She shook her head. "They don't have the classes I need. I have to go to a regular high school. And I can't go back to San Gabriel."

I remembered the vice principal's tirade and had to admit she was probably right. "What will you do then?" Even as I asked

I knew she wanted to go away. My hands felt suddenly cold. I wrapped them in the dishtowel I'd been using to dry the lunch dishes and sat next to her on the sofa.

"I'm going to San Bernardino, Mom. Aunt Rose looked into it, and they'll take me starting winter term. She says I should do it now, while the baby's young. If I wait too long, I'll never get it done."

I remembered Rose mentioning something on Thanksgiving about Libby coming to stay with them. I hadn't really paid much attention; there was so much going on at the time. In any case, I hadn't thought she meant so soon.

"When does winter term start?"

"In January, right after Christmas vacation. Aunt Rose says I can come anytime I want to, but I was thinking maybe Christmas Day. We'll be out there anyway. Jesse and I can just stay."

"It makes sense, Celia," Jake said later that night. "I think she's making a wise decision. We should be proud of her."

I knew I would miss Libby and the baby terribly, but I also knew he was right.

*   *   *

Jake's mother insisted on having the entire crew for Christmas Eve. "No offense, child, but your house is too small. Everyone is coming this year."

"I hope she's not too disappointed if Dave doesn't come," I said to Jake.

He shrugged. "Ma should know by now not to count on him. Besides, no one's heard a word since he got out of jail. Why would she expect him to come home?"

Because it's Christmas, and this is his home, I thought to myself.

*   *   *

Anne Marie arrived on the twenty-third. I was stirring up a batch of fudge and Libby was wrapping packages at the kitchen table when the phone rang. "I'll get it," she said, jumping up to answer it before the noise could wake the baby. I had no more than greased and floured my large sheet-cake pan when she popped back in the kitchen, grinning like she'd won first prize.

"Well, that didn't take long." I smiled back at her. "Who was it?"

"That," she said breathlessly, "was Aunt Anne. She said to tell you to put candles on the fudge. Uncle Chuck is here!"

I nearly dropped my spoon. "He came with her? Well, where is he? When did they arrive?"

Libby tied a triple-loop bow with a flourish and set the finished package on the chair. "Let's see," she pretended to think about her answers. "He came with Aunt Anne, they're both at Grandma Freeman's right now, but he's going to sleep at Uncle John's, and I think she said they just got there, but it could have been an hour ago, or maybe half an hour. No, it must be more like two because they would have had to get their bags and drive in from the airport. On the other hand, of course, maybe they—"

"All right, Miss Smarty Pants." I snapped a dishtowel in her direction. "Thank you for the information."

She gave a mock curtsy, gathered up an armful of packages and went to set them under the tree.

Jake came through the back door with an armload of pine boughs and a package of mistletoe. "Hi." He held the mistletoe over my head and kissed me, then stuck his finger in the cake batter.

"Jake Freeman, stop that!"

He raised his eyebrows. "Well, I'm insulted. You've never complained about my kisses before."

"You know very well what I mean."

I could see the devil in his eyes, but Libby came back into the kitchen and put an end to his shenanigans. "All right, you two. It's Christmas; no fighting, okay?"

I looked at her, astounded, "Liberty Jane, we weren't fighting."

Her father held up the mistletoe and kissed her on the cheek. "All right, sugar, we'll call a truce. I promise not to beat her until after Christmas."

She scowled. "That's not funny, Daddy."

Jake rolled his eyes and took the pine boughs in to decorate the windowsill. But Libby's comment upset me. I'd be the first to admit that we'd been a little short with each other lately, but that was only natural with the kind of pressure we'd been under. Goodness knows, our marriage wasn't all sweetness and light. But I'd always taken pride in the fact that we didn't fight like some other couples did.

Now wasn't the time or place, but I vowed to have a talk with Libby. Soon.

Chapter
Thirty-six

Dotty called at three o'clock on Christmas Eve. "I'm so glad you caught us," I told her. "We were just about to leave for the Freemans'."

"I'm glad too." She sounded down. "I miss you, girl, I really do. The holidays just haven't been the same this year." We chatted for a few minutes, then she said merry Christmas and gave the phone to Sam.

"Merry Christmas, doll. Put Jake on a minute, will you?"

I handed the phone to Jake and went in to help Libby with the baby.

Jake stayed quiet all the way to his mother's house. He glowered at the traffic and nearly missed the Freemont Avenue exit. When he sped through the yellow light at Sixth and Madison, I'd had enough.

"Darling, slow down. Dinner's not until five. No one's going to eat your share of pie."

Libby giggled from the back seat, but Jake didn't crack a smile. "I'm not worried about pie, Celia. Sam just told me some disturbing news. I need to check it out."

Dotty hadn't said anything was wrong. "Is it Dave again?"

I heard Libby shift behind us.

"No. At least I don't think he's involved." He pulled up to the curb and stopped the car. "I'll take care of it, okay?"

Take care of what? I covered my irritation by helping Libby gather up the baby's things while Jake dug the huge cardboard box of packages from the trunk of the car.

I tried to maneuver the birthday cake I'd made for Chuck into the crowded kitchen, but the counters were covered with Jell-O salads, deviled eggs, plates of relishes and three kinds of potatoes.

"Celia, dear, the cake is beautiful!" Ma Freeman kissed me on the cheek. "Put it on the sideboard in the dining room."

There were so many people to greet, I lost track of time. The men had all congregated outside, and the women scurried between the kitchen and the living room, where little Jesse was the center of attention. It was almost six when Ma finally rang the dinner bell.

Libby laid the baby in his portable crib and joined the noisy throng around the table. "Where's Daddy and Uncle Brian?" She was talking to me, but her voice must have carried, because the conversation round us stopped.

Ma looked confused. "Well, I'm sure they were here a minute ago."

John set his napkin on the table. "They're probably still out back. I'll go."

"Don't bother." Chuck was looking out the living-room window. "They went for a ride about forty-five minutes ago, and Jake's car's not here."

I frowned. "Are you sure? It's not like Jake to leave without telling anyone."

"Oh dear, I hope nothing's happened to them." Ma turned to John. "Maybe you should go and look for them."

I was about to echo her concern when Jake and Brian pulled up. They sat a moment, then got out of the car and walked toward the door. Halfway up the walk, Brian turned and started to cut across the grass, but Jake gripped his arm and guided him into the house.

"There you are," Ma scolded. "We were getting worried. Come sit down—" She stopped and studied her sons' faces.

The room was quiet. So quiet I could hear the baby's even breathing in the other room. No one moved, and every eye was fixed on the two men standing just inside the front door. Jake looked grim, and Brian's face was ashen. Like Papa's when the policemen took him off to jail. Like Uncle Edward's when they told him Billy had died. Like Pa Freeman in his open coffin.

"Brian," Ma said quietly, "are you ill?"

Brian shook his head, and Ma gave a short, sharp nod. "All right, then come and sit. We must thank God for this Christmas feast and eat before it gets cold. Whatever is wrong can wait." Her last words were directed at Jake.

They obeyed. As the oldest, Jake said grace. He ate a little of everything and listened to his family's forced conversation, but he spoke only when spoken to and refused to look at me at all. Brian looked like he wanted to bolt from the room. He kept his head down and only picked at his food.

"Well, I hate to interrupt this happy chatter," John spoke into the gloom, "but I do have some news, if anyone's interested."

Everyone looked at him but Brian.

"I hope it's good news," Sara's Steven said. "I think this family could use some."

John smiled, "Well, it is for me. The paper's sending me on assignment. I'm going to Vietnam with a group of other reporters to get the scoop on what's happening over there. They've given me my own photographer and an expense account."

"Hey, that's great!" Steven jumped up and shook his hand.

"Congratulations, John." Amy leaned over and kissed his cheek.

His mother beamed. "I always said you were the best reporter at that paper. Now you get to travel. Your pa would be proud of you."

"When do you leave?" Anne Marie spoke quietly, and I could tell she wasn't as excited as everyone else seemed to be.

"On the first. We catch a flight from New York, so I have to be out of here on New Year's Eve."

"I wish he wasn't going," Anne Marie whispered while we were doing dishes. "Things are heating up over there, and I don't mean just the weather."

"He is a reporter, not a soldier. Surely he'll be protected."

Anne gave me a weak smile and patted my hand. "Of course he will. Don't pay any attention to me."

Chuck stuck his head around the corner. "Are you girls about done? I think I'd like to walk off some of this food." He looked meaningfully at Anne.

"Go ahead. I'll finish up." I took the tea towel from her and wiped the last two plates.

"Come on, Libby, you too. A walk will do us all good. Celia, Jake wants you in the living room." Chuck peeked into Jesse's crib, then escorted Libby and Anne out the door.

It was close to seven o'clock. Sara June, Amy and their families were getting ready to leave. "It's a four-hour drive," Amy was saying when I joined them in the living room, "and we have to be at Stan's parents for dinner tomorrow."

Ma sat next to Jake and Brian on the sofa, wadding up a clean white hankie. John stood, hands tucked in the pockets of his slacks, staring out the living-room window.

Just as Chuck opened the front door, the neighbor's cat, a lean, white shorthair named Lightning, leaped from the branches of the maple tree, snagged a sparrow in midflight and plummeted to the ground. For a moment none of us moved. The cat turned his head toward the open door, twitched his tail, then trotted off into the bushes with his prize.

"Don't go." Brian's voice cracked, and he had to clear his throat twice before he could continue. "I have something to say, and you might as well all hear it."

Libby looked at her father. She was used to being excused from adult conversations, but Jake motioned us both to come sit beside him. Brian had moved forward, elbows on his knees, his head buried in his hands. I took the spot next to Jake, and Libby perched on the armrest next to me. Everyone else either sat where they were or stood awkwardly around the edges of the room.

Brian lifted his head and looked around the room. His gaze finally shifted to his mother, and his eyes locked onto hers. "You were right, Ma. Dave never took Pa's money out of that well," he said evenly. "I did."

Chapter
Thirty-seven

The candlelight service at Westside Presbyterian reminded me
more of Pa Freeman's funeral than a celebration of the birth
of Christ. We sang "Silent Night" and "Joy to the World," but
our family's faces reflected more gloom than joy in the flicker-
ing light.

Jake clutched my hand in the half-darkness. Down the row,
Chuck and Anne were holding hands as well. Libby sat on my
left, cradling little Jesse, whose peaceful sleep went undisturbed by the voices around him. Ma sat between Brian and
John, her head held high and her voice ringing with conviction
as she sang, "Joy to the earth, the Savior reigns." When we filed
out, Brian was crying openly. Even Chuck's face was streaked
with tears.

We had packed the car before we left the Freemans' so we
could head straight home after the service. We had another
drive to San Bernardino on Christmas Day. I brought up Sam's
phone call on the way. "How did Sam know?" I asked.

Jake shook his head. "He didn't. When he phoned today, he
told me they had broken a multimillion-dollar crime ring, some
mob-related money-interest scam. Brian's name was on a list
of victims. Sam and his people were supposed to contact them

to see if they would testify. Sam suspected we didn't know about it, so he called. He wants me to encourage Brian to testify. They want to put these thugs away for a very long time." He pulled into the driveway and shut off the engine.

Libby crawled out of the car and lifted Jesse to her shoulder. "I'm going to put the baby down and go to bed." She sniffed. "I hope someone plans on contacting Uncle Dave. He should know his name's been cleared."

Jake rested his forehead against the steering wheel, and I massaged his shoulder. I could tell by the way he moved his arm that he was in pain.

He sat up and smacked the dashboard with his fist. "Doggone it, Celia, I should have seen it. Brian's been acting squirrelly ever since Pa died. Dumping Pam and doing all those things for Ma. He never wanted to talk about Dave either, and he tried to keep John and me away from the well that day. He kept insisting it was all a hoax, or if Pa had any money, he'd lost it a long time ago. I almost believed him. But then we found the empty can. And to me, Dave had sealed his guilt by running away. How blind could I be?"

"Not blind, darling," I tried to reassure him. "Just logical."

I didn't add that I'd believed Dave after Miguel's parents had brought that letter. And I'd wondered about Brian's behavior, but it never dawned on me he might have actually taken the money.

Brian had confessed the whole thing. "I'd taken some heavy losses at a poker game—more than one, actually. I couldn't pay my debts, so I borrowed money from this friend of a friend. It turned out they wanted the money back with 40 percent interest. When the time was up, I couldn't pay. They gave me two more weeks and upped the interest to 50 percent. I was scared. I knew I could never come up with that kind of cash.

"I went to the house that day, the day Dave left for Mexico.

I saw his bike in the drive and figured he was up to something, so I snuck into the house. I saw him through the kitchen window, running from the back lot. He jumped on his bike and took off. Pa's letter was on the kitchen table. I read it and wanted to rip Dave apart. I figured he'd grabbed the money and run off, but I decided to check, just in case.

"When I found the cash still in that stupid can, all I could think was that here was my salvation. There was enough to pay the debt and more. So I took it. I didn't think twice about it. Not then." His voice had faltered, and his gaze shifted from his mother to the floor.

"I went right out and bought Pam a wedding ring. Then I called my contact and told him I had the money. He asked how much, and, like an idiot, I told him. 'Imagine that,' he said. 'That's exactly how much your life is worth.' "

Brian's voice had dropped almost to a whisper then. He met his mother's gaze. "I'm sorry, Ma. It's gone, all of it. But I'll take care of you. I'll work until the day I die to see that you don't want for anything."

* * *

Sometimes the hardest things to do are the ones that turn out best for everybody. It nearly broke my heart to kiss Libby and the baby goodby on Christmas night. Aunt Rose assured me they'd be fine—and I didn't doubt it for a minute—but like I told Jake on the way home, "I feel like we're deserting her. Or at least shirking our responsibility."

"Celia, we've been all through this fifty times. Libby needs to finish her education and get on with the life she's chosen for herself. At least she's with family. We should be thankful Edward is willing to take them on."

I knew he was right. If Libby needed a chance to spread her wings, Aunt Rose and Uncle Edward's home was the best launching pad in town. But I knew I would miss her and little

Chapter Thirty-seven

Jesse terribly.

Working on the project with Stuart kept me busy several hours each day. I met and interviewed families who had adopted children, as well as the grown-up children themselves. Most of the young people thought their adoption files should be available to them on request. One young woman who had just turned twenty-one expressed the feelings of the majority: "It doesn't mean we don't love the parents who raised us. We just want a chance to know our roots. I don't really care about meeting my birth parents so much as I want to know who they are. Do I have siblings, grandparents, an inherited talent or a tendency toward some disease? Those are the questions I would ask. It would give me a better sense of my own identity."

The adoptive parents weren't so sure. "It hurts my feelings," one of them confided. "I'm the one who changed his diapers and stayed up with him all night when he had the flu. My husband coached him in Little League and tutored him when he was failing math. Why is he so keen to find his 'real' parents? We *are* his real parents."

By the end of March 1963 we'd interviewed over fifty families. With very few exceptions, the adoptions had been a positive experience for all concerned. We never found another experience like Chuck's.

* * *

Anne Marie called on April 1. "I had to let you know, Chuck is gone," she said. "He sold his Corvette and emptied his bank account. Then he bought a souped-up Harley and just split. He called me two nights ago to say he had some business to attend to down south, and he needed time to think."

"Oh Anne," I cried, "I'm so sorry. I thought—I mean, you two were doing so well together. When he came with you at Christmas, he seemed happy. I thought surely . . ."

"Me too. He's changed, Celia, he really has. Since the baby

was born he's been so loving and much more open to spiritual things." She took a deep breath and continued. "I don't know what he's up to, but whatever it is can't be permanent. I got a call this morning from a banker. He said to tell Mr. Summers that the loan on the restaurant went through."

Someday I'm going to own it, Chuck had told me that day on the waterfront. "He bought Arturo's?"

"That would be my guess. He'll be back, Celia. I know he will."

"I'll call you if I hear from him," I promised. "And if he shows up here, I'll send him home where he belongs!"

"Not until he's ready, Celia. He has to want to be here."

"Okay, I promise not to make a fuss." I hung up wondering what my brother could be up to now.

* * *

Desegregation of universities and public buildings in the South continued. The Reverend Martin Luther King Jr. was arrested in Birmingham, Alabama. Women were granted the right to equal pay for equal work. The months sped by, and still there had been no word from Dave or Chuck.

Miguel's family wrote from time to time, enclosing a few dollars and expressing their desire to see their grandson. Libby agreed to a visit, and Jake offered to pay their train fare up for Jesse's first birthday. Miguel himself never came. But each month Libby received a check from him for twenty or thirty dollars. "It does help," she said, "and little Jesse deserves it."

Libby graduated in June. She didn't wear a cap and gown or walk across the stage with the rest of the San Bernardino High School class of 1963, but she had her diploma just the same. The week before her nineteenth birthday, she landed a job as a receptionist in a dental office.

"Only four hours a day, but at least I can help with some expenses, and I get to spend more time with Jesse," she told us.

Anne Marie called back on the Fourth of July to wish Libby happy birthday and tell us Chuck was home. "He got back a few days ago. Let me put it this way: he has a lot to tell you."

"Hi, sis," Chuck broke in. "Did Anne tell you she finally came to her senses and agreed to marry me? I knew she couldn't resist my boyish charm forever." I heard Anne giggle in the background. "Anyway, we tie the knot tomorrow. We'd invite you to the wedding, but we've waited too long as it is, so it's just us and the preacher at the First Presbyterian Church."

I was speechless, which was just as well because Anne recaptured the receiver. "Celia? I know this must be a shock. Look, tell everyone we love them and we'll be down for a visit after we get back from our honeymoon. Sometime in the next few weeks, okay?"

"Anne Marie Freeman, what about—" I wanted to ask if she had explained all this to anyone else—like her mother, or Flo and Jerry, but I heard a buzz and realized I was talking to dead air.

"What was that all about?" Jake frowned over the edge of the morning *Examiner.*

I pulled out a dining-room chair and sat down to catch my breath. "I guess we'll find out in a few weeks," I said.

* * *

September. Jake took me out to dinner for my birthday. Sam and Dotty wired flowers and mailed a package of cards from the children. Zeke's and Mikey's had been made with scraps of crepe and construction paper. Mike had not spared the glue or crayons, and the result looked more like a collage than a birthday card. I cried and taped it to the refrigerator.

Little Jesse turned one year old the next day. I marveled at the way his strong legs propelled his solid body across the floor and his chubby hands patiently plucked the ribbons and bows off his presents. "Me." He beamed and pulled away when Libby tried to help him.

"I can't believe this," I told Aunt Rose. "Libby never walked or said a word until she was almost two."

Aunt Rose smiled. "He's a smart one. He can empty a cupboard faster than I can put things away. And he knows when it's time for Libby to come home. He toddles to the front door and sits until he hears her car, then he hollers 'Ma ma ma ma ma' until she comes in and picks him up."

We hadn't had a response from the Floreses until the end of July. Then Libby had received a huge package and a birthday card with a letter inside. "We've decided not to come," the letter read. "Estelle es afraid she will become too attached, and her heart will break when we will leave again. It is better if we do not come at all."

Libby tried to hold back her tears. "I feel sorry for them, Mom," she said when she called. "And wait until you see what they sent Jesse."

The gift turned out to be a rocking horse, hand carved and hand painted, with a hand-stitched leather saddle and an embroidered halter and bridle that only Estelle could have made.

"He loves it," Aunt Rose confided. "The first time we tried to take him off it, he threw such a fit we had to let him rock himself to sleep and catch him before he fell."

*   *   *

Later in the month Governor George Wallace was forced to give in, and the University of Alabama allowed the first Negroes ever into its sacred halls.

"It's about time they paid attention to the nation's constitution," Jake commented. "It says all men are created equal, and that doesn't mean just in the North."

"I'm glad you feel that way," I said and sat down next to him on the sofa. "That was your mother on the phone. Your brother Dave is on his way over here, and Miguel is with him."

Chapter
Thirty-eight

It seemed strange to see Dave behind the wheel of Brian's VW. His face and arms were as brown as the young man next to him, and his muscles bulged beneath the rolled-up sleeves of his T-shirt.

Dave and Miguel got out of the car and moved toward the house. Miguel was dressed in an identical white T-shirt and black cotton dungarees. He was shorter than Dave but even more handsome, and I couldn't help noticing his eyes. Sparkling bright, and black as coal. Jesse's eyes. Jesse's brows and long, curved lashes. The tiny dimple just below the cheekbone. There could be no doubt this was our grandson's father.

Jake had to have seen it too, but when he opened the front door, he kept his eyes on Dave and nodded toward the car. "Where's Brian?" His voice held a challenge, and Dave smiled.

"Not in a hospital, if that's what you're thinking." He shook his head. "Brian's fine, man. He's with Pam. They have her car, so Bri said I could borrow his." He paused, then nodded toward his companion. "We won't bug you for long. Miguel here has something he wants to say."

Miguel had been studying his feet, but now he looked up at Jake and held out his hand. Jake hesitated a moment, then shook it. "My name is Miguel Flores, Mr. Freeman, and I have come to tell you how sorry I am for what I have done to your family."

"Sometimes," Jake said slowly, "sorry just isn't enough."

Dave's face turned red, but Miguel nodded. "I know that, sir. I have come to ask your forgiveness, even though I don't expect you to grant it."

I touched Jake's shoulder and pushed the door open wider. "Jake, where are your manners?" I said nervously. "Don't keep them standing on the porch. Dave, Miguel, please come in and have something to drink."

Dave shook his head. "Not now, Celia. Maybe another time." He was talking to me, but he looked straight at Jake. "We're on our way to San Bernardino to see Libby and the baby. Rose has invited us to dinner." He gave Jake a mock salute. "See you later, brother. We'll be around awhile." He turned and walked back to the car.

Miguel ducked his head and followed.

"Jake Freeman, that was rude!" I said when he had shut the door behind them. "You didn't give them a chance."

Now Jake's face turned red. "Don't start on me, Celia." He grabbed a Coke from the fridge and bolted out the back door.

* * *

Jake tossed and turned most of the night, keeping both of us awake. He came to the breakfast table but didn't have much to say beyond a polite "Good morning" and "Please pass the syrup."

We went to church as usual, but he pulled away when I tried to take his hand during the sermon. We hurried out the side door as soon as Pastor Willis said the final amen.

I fixed fried-egg sandwiches for lunch, then, while Jake was engrossed in the ball game, called Libby on the phone.

"It was good to see him, Mom," she said softly. "And I know

he's proud of little Jesse. He played with him for hours. Uncle Dave did too, and Jesse loved it."

I held my breath, half expecting her to say she and Miguel were getting back together. I'd been thinking about it since yesterday's visit and had mixed feelings. On the one hand, it would be good for Libby to be married to her baby's father, and little Jesse should have two parents. On the other hand, I doubted if Miguel could support them. And what if she moved to Mexico? We'd never get to see them. And then, of course, there was Jake.

"Mother? Are you listening?"

"Oh, I'm sorry, Libby, what were you saying?"

"I said, isn't it neat that Uncle Chuck went all the way down to Ensenada? He told Uncle Dave about Uncle Brian and showed them pictures of the baby. Didn't they tell you? That's what made them come. Uncle Dave sold his bike and they hitchhiked all the way."

"Chuck went down?"

"Mother, honestly, maybe you should take a nap or something. Haven't you heard a word I've been saying?"

I hung up and dialed Anne Marie.

She answered on the second ring. "Yes, Chuck went to Ensenada. Here, I'll let you talk to him."

Chuck came on the line. "Hi, sis, sorry we haven't made it to L.A., but you know how it is—married bliss and all."

Married bliss? I'd forgotten what that was like.

"Actually," he continued, "I've been busy at the restaurant, and Anne has been working double shifts. Maybe we'll make it for Thanksgiving."

He went on to tell me he'd visited the DuVals in San Diego. "I apologized," he said quietly. "I knew that's what God wanted me to do. They didn't accept, but it doesn't matter. I've done my part."

"I'm glad," I said. And it was the truth. Even though Chuck had refused to participate in Stuart's study, I was happy he had finally made peace with his past.

I wanted to ask what had changed his mind about saying yes to God, but I didn't think it was the time or place. In fact, it wasn't until 1965, when Chuck and Anne adopted their first child, that I learned what had happened to change my brother's heart.

"It was a combination of things, Cissy," Chuck told me as he bounced Kim Sung, renamed Timmy, on his knee. "Anne's steadfast faith in God was one. She never compromised and never gave up on me. Then there was your devotion to Libby when she got in trouble, and little Jesse's birth. That was a miracle—one I couldn't deny." He set the squirming baby in the playpen. "But the kicker was Jake's family. The way they rallied around Brian when he spilled his guts that day. That was love, sis, pure and simple. I knew it came from God, and I knew I wanted some of it for me."

* * *

On October 2, 1963, Sandy Koufax retired fifteen players in the opening game of the World Series, and by October 6 the Dodgers had accomplished the impossible: they took the series from the Yankees in just four games. I thought Jake was having a heart attack right there on the living-room floor.

When he finally calmed down enough to speak, he went to the phone and dialed Uncle Edward. "I never thought I'd see the day," he said. "I guess the Dodgers are the team to beat." And with that sentence he erased a lifelong loyalty to the New York Yankees.

* * *

Aunt Rose had finally gone to the doctor toward the end of September. By October we knew the news wasn't good.

"It's such a nuisance," she told me on the phone that day.

"But the specialist insists I have surgery right away. He says the tumor is small, and he thinks we've caught it soon enough. I don't want you to worry, dear."

I couldn't help worrying. *Cancer* was a whispered word. A death sentence. The demon disease. All I could think to say was "When?"

"Wednesday morning. But I don't want you to come, unless Libby needs you, of course. I'll be in the hospital just a couple of days, and there's not a thing you can do."

We went to the hospital, of course. Jake drove me over the day she came home, so Libby could go back to work.

"Flat as a pancake," Aunt Rose joked. "But never mind. As soon as I can wear the prosthesis, no one will be able to tell."

I sighed. "At least they got it all. That's good news. Are you sure the doctor said you could get up so soon?"

"Soon! I've been down two weeks. You go on home and finish your research project. I've got Libby, and Edward can mind little Jesse. The hardest part for me is that I can't pick him up."

* * *

The United States and Russia had finally made a pact to ban above-ground testing of nuclear missiles. But you couldn't trust the communists to keep their word.

"They don't trust us either," John had said when they installed a hot line from Washington, D.C., to the Kremlin. "Kennedy and Khrushchev can be in touch at a moment's notice," he added. "But don't kid yourselves. All either one of them has to do is push a button and the other country goes up in smoke."

John had been back from Vietnam a week. We knew the president had sent in more advisers. "Right," John explained sarcastically, "sixteen thousand unarmed soldiers." John's next few articles were scathing reports of mayhem and bloodshed in South Vietnam, "which no amount of U.S. intervention could deter."

"I'm getting worried, Celia," Dotty said on the phone one day. "David's almost seventeen. What will it be like when he's old enough to go to war?"

I shuddered. "That's a long way off. Let's not think about it now."

Chapter
Thirty-nine

November 22, 1963. I took the bus to work as usual that morning. When I left the house, the fog was so thick I couldn't even count the sidewalk cracks. I kept my eyes on the faint flashes of red, yellow and green, and let the new traffic signal at the corner of Valley and Wells guide me to my stop.

Forty-five minutes later I climbed the two flights of stairs to Stuart's office, grabbed a stack of folders to file and turned on the TV.

The president was in Dallas that day, campaigning for re-election. John Fitzgerald Kennedy, the nation's favorite son.

Jackie sits beside him, squinting into the sun. She has on a pink coat, obviously wool, and a hat to match. The convertible top on the shiny blue Lincoln is down, and she brushes a strand of brown hair from her eyes. Both Kennedys are smiling and waving to the cheering crowd. It makes me want to cheer and wave right back.

Then, a loud pop, like a car backfiring. The president raises both hands, turns his head toward his wife, then slumps toward her on the seat. The camera jumps and spins this way and that. Men suddenly are running everywhere.

Jackie stands up and holds her hand out to a man who is trying to climb over the back of the moving car. He shoves her back, then drags himself over the trunk and into the seat.

We didn't see it all until much later, of course. After they released the newsreel film. But hearing about it was just as shocking.

I had just bent down to file a folder under *W* for Wilson, when I heard the announcer gasp. "Ladies and gentlemen, we have reports of gunfire. It appears the president may have been shot."

I stood there horrified. Too stunned to retrieve another folder that had fallen at my feet. I hadn't heard Stuart come into the room, but I realized he was standing behind me, watching over my shoulder. We stood closed-mouthed and hardly breathing while reporters scrambled to fill the airwaves with what little they knew.

Finally Walter Cronkite, his face pale, his voice intense, confirmed the rumors. "In Dallas, Texas, three shots were fired at President Kennedy's motorcade. First reports say the president was seriously wounded by this shooting."

I felt Stuart's hands steady my shoulders. This could not be happening. Not in America. Not in 1963.

The reports were sporadic: "Apparently three bullets were found." "Governor Connally also appears to have been wounded." "A bullet entered the throat . . ." "Blood transfusions . . ." "A priest has administered last rites."

Cameras flashed between Parkland Hospital and people on the street who babbled breathlessly about what they had seen and heard.

The chaos continued for half an hour. Then we watched as Mr. Cronkite, choking on the words, delivered the news: "President John Fitzgerald Kennedy was pronounced dead at approximately 1:00 p.m. Central Standard Time today in Dallas."

* * *

People react to grief in all kinds of ways, I told myself later, *most of them too private or too foolish to behold.* I remember thinking how grateful I was that no one else was around to see what happened next.

I don't remember crying out, but Stuart gripped my shoulders harder, then released them as he turned me around. I pressed my face into the hollow of his neck just below his starched white collar. I felt cold, shaky cold, and his body was so warm. His arms tightened, pulling me closer. A heartbeat later, he bent his head to mine.

His kiss was searching-soft, then demanding. The heat arched through me, as sharp and painful as lightning, then flowed warm and sweet until I thought I would dissolve.

I should have pulled away. Instead, I clung to him until my knees gave way. He lowered me gently to the sofa. He began to sit down beside me, but the touch of cool Naugahyde nudged my sense of propriety and I pushed him gently away. "Stuart, no. Please, we mustn't."

He released me instantly and straightened up. When we could both breathe again, he walked over to a cabinet behind his desk and returned with a decanter of brandy. Neither of us said a word as he filled two glasses and handed one to me.

I'd had liquor only once before, not counting the time when Jake and I were young and he'd found Papa's bottle in the shed. This had been after we were married, at a party for a friend of Jake's. I hadn't liked it much.

Now I took a cautious sip of the drink Stuart handed me. It was surprisingly sweet. I took another sip and felt the amber liquid warm me all the way from my throat down to my toes. This time the fire revived me. I tried to stand, but my legs still wouldn't hold, so I scooted to the edge of the couch.

"Stuart," I began, but he put his finger softly to my lips.

"Shh. It's all right, Celia. Don't say a thing." He finished his drink, then poured another. I shook my head when he offered to refill mine. He ran a hand through his hair, pushing it back from his forehead. He started to speak again, then turned away and walked over to the window.

I knew the view from there; I'd studied it a thousand times; stately red-brick buildings, the wide expanse of grass broken by winding walkways and wind-bent trees. Right now the campus would be deserted. Everyone would be inside watching the news, trying to figure out exactly what was happening and why.

Like Stuart Haley and Celia Freeman.

Stuart sighed, and I thought I saw his shoulders tremble. He kept his back to me when he spoke again. His voice held sadness and a strong resolve. "I apologize, Celia. I don't know what got into me. The turmoil of the moment, I would guess."

I nodded, though I knew he couldn't see me. Turmoil was an understatement for my feelings right then, but I knew two things for sure: my relationship with Stuart Haley had just changed, and I'd better get on home to Jake.

"Would you please take me home?" I said. "I don't think I can make it on the bus."

Later, we agreed that our momentary passion had been an accident. A nervous reaction to the terrible events we had just witnessed. But I knew in my heart that wasn't so. There'd been something between us from the beginning, when the handsome young professor rescued the lady-lost, just like in a fairy tale.

Seven years. We'd been so careful not to let it show. Grandma Eva always said, "A watched pot never boils." I guess, just for a moment, we forgot to watch the pot.

* * *

That night I lay staring at the ceiling. I'd taken one of the sedatives the doctor had given me before little Jess was born, but it had backfired, leaving me foggy-headed, restless and awake.

It had been a quiet evening. Jake had telephoned Uncle Edward before dinner and learned that they were all just fine. "Shaken, of course. With all his faults, he was a darn good president."

Then Aunt Rose got on the phone, and I could almost see her shake her head. "What is this world coming to? And his poor little wife!"

"I'm scared, Mom," Libby said, sniffling. "If they can kill the president, nobody's safe. I'm scared for my baby."

"Nobody's going to hurt Jesse," I soothed. "Do you want us to come and get you?"

I heard her hesitate, then sigh. "No. It's all right. Jess is asleep. Besides, I have to work tomorrow."

Aunt Rose came back on the line. "Don't you worry, dear. We're all just fine. The doctor says I'm healing beautifully, and the last blood test was negative. We have a lot to be thankful for, even in this horrible time."

I hung up knowing my daughter and grandchild were in good hands.

The sleeping pill was finally starting to take effect. I closed my eyes, supposing I would dream of Stuart Haley's kiss. Instead, I saw Mama in her pink silk robe, sitting at the kitchen table of our house in Pike, Nevada. She was sipping coffee from a china cup and laughing at one of Roy Cummings's jokes.

Roy sat in Papa's chair, big as you please, stirring sugar into Papa's mug. He handed me and Susi a dollar each and said, "Take Krista to the carnival."

Mama's laugh this time was short and low. "Be good," she said. "Be good and don't let go of Krista's hand." She was talking to me, but her eyes never left Roy Cummings's face.

Chapter
Forty

Sometimes love is an illusion, light and shadow, finger rabbits on a whitewashed wall.

I never meant to fall in love with Stuart Haley. After all, Jake was my husband, and even through the bad times I'd never stopped loving him. But Stuart praised my work, admired the new blouse I bought at May Co. and complimented me when I got my hair trimmed. Jake only noticed if the roast beef was overdone. Stuart talked to me. Not just "Did you see the Dodgers beat the Giants?" He asked my opinions on literature, campus politics and world affairs. When things had started going wrong with Libby, he'd been the one who listened to my fears and helped me through the hardest parts.

For the moment, I tried to set my jumbled thoughts and feelings aside.

Jake and I spent the weekend watching coverage of the assassination and its aftermath. For some reason, Kennedy's death was personal, like losing Papa and Mama and Jake's pa all over again. We cried not just for his family and ourselves, but for the death of something sacred. America and her hard-won freedoms had been laid to rest with the body of our president, and not even in the resurrection would it ever be whole again.

Jake and I went to Uncle Edward's on Sunday after church. We couldn't believe our eyes when Lee Harvey Oswald, Kennedy's accused killer, was murdered right there on TV. Libby ran and gathered little Jess. She held him so tightly he cried, and she had to let him down.

No one went to work on Monday. Jake even called Ron and told him not to come to the shop. "Stay home with your family," he said. "We'll get to that brake job tomorrow."

By nine o'clock that night our eyes were blurry from emotion, too much TV and not enough sleep. Jake flipped off the set, but instead of saying, "Man, I'm beat, I'm going to turn in," like I expected him to, he suggested we take a walk.

Jake didn't say a word for the first several minutes, and I was content to walk beside him and count the stars. The weather had finally cooled, and I was glad for the comfortable knit cardigan he had bought me last Christmas. Glad, too, to be out of the house and able to breathe the fresh night air.

Jake finally broke the silence. "Look, Celia, we need to talk." He took my arm and steered me back the way we'd come. "I'd like to go up to the lake for a while. Ron has an old fishing cabin up there. He said I could use it anytime."

I wrinkled my nose. "A fishing cabin? Jake, I couldn't. Christmas is only a few weeks away. And besides, Stuart's project is almost completed. I can't quit on him now."

He stopped still in the middle of the sidewalk, and I had to turn around to face him. The look on his face raised goosebumps on my arms. "Don't worry. I wouldn't dream of taking you away from your lover. I'm going to the lake alone."

Tiny fingers of ice crawled up my back and wrapped around my chest in a frozen grip until I could hardly breathe. I tried to speak, but my vocal chords were frozen too, in spite of the heat radiating from my face.

"Flo saw you the other day." He took my arm and propelled

me down the sidewalk, toward the house. "Don't worry, I covered for you. I told her Haley was just comforting you, and I already knew all about it."

"Jake," I gasped, "you're hurting me." He let go of my arm, and I rushed on. "Don't you see? That's exactly what did happen."

I thought he was going to hit me. Instead, he dropped his arms to his sides. "Please don't insult my intelligence by denying it. I've suspected something for a long time. Any idiot can see how you feel about him." He looked at me then, and the hurt I saw in his eyes was worse than any physical blow.

"Jake, please, let me—"

He held up his hand. "No. Don't say anything right now. We both have a lot of thinking to do. It's better if I go. It's been a rough two years for both of us. Just tell everyone I needed to get away for a while. It'll be the truth. And it will give you time to make some decisions."

He walked on with long, determined strides that took him to our door a good five minutes ahead of me. By the time I caught up, he was sitting in the driver's seat of his Impala. When he saw I was safely home, he started the engine and backed down the drive. It dawned on me as he pulled away that his suitcase had already been packed and waiting.

Somehow I made it through the next two weeks. After three days of calling in sick, I gave up and went back to work. Flo avoided me, and Stuart treated me like a hothouse orchid, bringing me coffee and telling me to take a break every five minutes. When he threatened to call Jake and tell him I needed to see a doctor, I confessed that Jake wasn't there. "He knows about the other day," I said. "Florence saw us and told him, and neither of them will let me explain."

Stuart looked away. "I'm sorry, Celia. The last thing I want is to see you hurt. If you want to quit, I'll understand."

"I can't quit now; we're too close to the end. Besides, wouldn't that just make it look like they're right?"

"Right about what?"

"Jake and Flo both think there's something between us. We have to show them they're wrong."

"Are they?" His voice was quiet, and I realized he was standing close. So close I could count the tiny dots on his tie and see the chafe marks where he had shaved that morning.

I tried to say, "Of course they're wrong, I'm a married woman and I love my husband," but I couldn't get the words out.

Stuart broke the spell. "I'll straighten things out with Florence." He handed me a slip of paper with a name and address stamped on the front. "This is the last interview. Why don't you take my car, go talk to this woman, then meet me at the Coffee Mill for lunch?"

I almost told him no. Having lunch together would just add fuel to the fire. *But,* I reasoned, *we've been meeting for lunch for years. To stop now might look even more suspicious.*

I took the keys and stumbled down the stairs. *Oh Lord, I'm so tired and confused. What am I going to do?* There was no powerful insight, no instant response. I realized it was the first prayer I'd uttered in weeks and felt a rush of fear. *Please, God, don't you leave me too.*

Dotty would have given me a healthy shake and told me how pitiful I sounded. Then we'd have had a heart to heart, and she would have helped me work it through. But Dotty wasn't there. And the last thing I wanted was to try and explain all this long distance.

* * *

There's an old saying, "Absence makes the heart grow fonder." But evidently that wasn't true for Jake and me. For years I'd woken up next to him, poured his morning coffee and kissed him hello-goodby. I missed those rituals, but as the days went by I was appalled at how little my routine had changed. I realized that for the last few years anyway, he had never really been there. To be fair, I'd had my work and our home to run. And I'm sure Jake never meant it to happen any more than I did. But the truth was we'd become like strangers living in the same house.

Did I love him? Certainly not with the same intense feelings that I had for Stuart. Jake and I had shared that ardor once, but not for a long time. I thought our love had just grown stronger, more mature. Now I understood that we had let it get stale.

Every empty night the questions raged: Could I give Jake up? Was I willing to ignore the pull of passion and settle for contentment? How could I condone doing otherwise? I knew without a doubt that God wouldn't.

Flo called me on a Sunday afternoon three weeks before Christmas. "Jerry and I are having our party next Saturday night. I know it's earlier than usual, but we've got other plans for the next three weekends."

"I don't know, Flo. Jake's not back yet, and under the circumstances, I don't think I should come alone."

She went quiet for a minute, then I heard her take a long, deep breath and let it out again. "Celia, Stuart told me all the trouble I caused by calling Jake. I just thought that if he knew how things were, he would start paying more attention to you and try to win you back."

I was shocked. Had my needs been that transparent? "How could you think that, Flo? You gave Jake the impression Stuart and I were having an affair. And whether or not you want to believe it, that's not true!"

"I know." Her voice cracked. "I'm sorry, Celia. You and Jake have always had such a great marriage. I thought all it needed was a kick in the rear. Anyway," she sniffed, "you can't deny that you and Stuart more than like each other. No one kisses a casual friend that way."

I sighed. "We'll work it out, Flo. But I don't know about the party. You'd better not count on us this year."

By that Friday night I was feeling lonely, restless, angry and afraid. Jake hadn't written or called, and it made me furious that he wasn't willing to listen to my side. Having to skirt around questions from the family didn't make my life any easier. "Have you heard from Jake, dear?" Aunt Rose asked when I called to check on them. "I'm sure you miss him. Will he be home soon?"

"I don't know," I said truthfully. "I guess that depends on how many fish he's caught." *And what kind of decisions he's made,* I thought.

She went on to tell me that Libby was on a date. "With a nice young man she met at church. His parents are lovely people," she said enthusiastically. "We've known them for years."

I couldn't help feeling annoyed. "Do you think she should be dating again so soon? Jesse's only fifteen months old."

She paused, then said quietly, "Don't worry, sweetheart. I know Libby will . . . She'll be fine. I think it's good for her to get out around young people again."

She was right, of course. Anyway, Libby was nineteen. She had to make her own decisions. *And,* my conscience shouted, *you are not one to talk!*

I hung up feeling like I'd gone two rounds with Sonny Liston. My forehead was damp with sweat, and I ached all over. "I think I'll go run a hot bath," I said aloud, then burst into tears when I realized there was no one to hear me.

Chapter
Forty-one

A nice long soak did wonders for my muscles but not my disposition. I could feel myself dissolving back into self-pity, so I turned the faucet knob to cold and stood shivering under the icy spray until my body and my brain were numb. I had just stepped into a long-sleeved flannel nightgown and stirred some instant Sanka into a cup of boiling water when the phone rang.

"Jake!" My heart pounded, but not in fear. "Where are you? When are you coming home?"

He was silent, and for a few long seconds my fear returned. When he finally spoke, his voice was quiet, cautious, like a novice swimmer standing on the edge of a clear, deep pool. "I'm coming home tomorrow, if that's all right with you."

"It's fine," I stammered. "I mean, I want you to."

"I'll be there around five. Ron is coming up in the morning. We're going fishing, then we have to stop by the shop."

How could he act like everything was so normal?

"Anything going on I should know about?"

Yes! I wanted to scream, *I'm on the verge of a nervous breakdown, Libby's probably dating Jack the Ripper, and Florence is throwing a big party.* "Florence and Jerry are having their Christmas party tomorrow night," I finally said. "I told her we wouldn't be there."

"I don't know, Celia; maybe we should. I don't want her spreading any rumors."

"She already has." I couldn't keep the poison from my voice. "She has you believing Stuart and I were having an affair!"

"I never said that. Look, this is not the time or place. I'll call you tomorrow afternoon when we get to the shop. Be ready to go, just in case, okay?"

"Fine." I said, feeling more sorry for myself than ever.

* * *

Saturday morning I got up exhausted but determined. I dug my best dress out of the closet and tore away the plastic cleaner's bag. It was a black, spaghetti-strap sheath, with a knee-length skirt and a million sequins on the bodice. I hadn't worn it since two years ago September, when Jake had taken me out to dinner for my birthday. "You look stunning," he had said back then. I slipped it on, hoping he would still feel the same.

Are you wearing this for Jake, or Stuart Haley?

Jake, of course, I told myself and pushed the thought away.

By four o'clock I had teased my hair in front and pushed the back into a high chignon. I pulled a few wisps forward into feather bangs, gave it a good coat of hairspray and slipped out of the bathrobe I'd worn to protect the dress.

The woman in my mirror surprised me. Her freckles had faded with her summer tan, and her skin looked like new-poured cream against the blackness of the dress. Her eyes glowed luminous blue from under darkened lashes, and her cheeks blushed with the help of Estee Lauder's Midnight Rose. Except for a few small lines around the mouth and neck, she looked ten years younger than her age. Stunning, but delicate. No, *fragile* was a better word. And I knew it would take very little to shatter her façade.

Jake called at five sounding tired. "I'm still at the shop, and it looks like we'll be another hour at least. Why don't you go on to the party? I'll change and meet you there."

"I'd rather wait for you."

"There's no need for that. Besides, Flo will be upset if we're both late for dinner."

The dinner was a buffet, and if I knew Flo, there would be plenty of food and drink to last the night. But I didn't want to argue. "All right, I'll meet you there," I conceded.

* * *

Florence met me at the door, eyebrows raised when she didn't see Jake.

"He's coming," I said, handing her my coat.

"Whoa! Who's the knockout in the slinky black dress? Flo, you didn't tell me you had a younger sister." Jerry's eyes were bright with mischief—and maybe just a bit too much champagne.

Flo smacked him on the shoulder. "All right, Romeo, go hang up Celia's coat." She turned to me. "Celia, I think you know almost everybody here. Be a doll and mingle, will you? I have to get some more crab puffs out of the oven."

Flo and Jerry's new house sat on a hill overlooking Pasadena. The huge living room was crowded with people laughing and talking and moving in and out of the dining room, where, as I'd expected, an opulent buffet decorated the side wall. On the far end, French doors led to an outside terrace with bench seats and potted palms. A steep flight of concrete stairs descended to the yard below.

Someone handed me a glass of champagne. I sipped it automatically as I searched the room, picking out familiar faces and trying to decide which group to join. Several of the men smiled appreciatively. Their wives glanced up, then looked quickly away.

I felt suddenly uncomfortable and wished I had either worn

my white bolero jacket or waited for Jake. *Or maybe I should have done both,* I decided, and set the drink down on the nearest table.

"The most beautiful woman in the room should not be standing by herself." Stuart's low voice was almost in my ear.

"Stuart, you startled me!"

"And you, me." His gaze traveled from my bodice to my shoes, and I felt myself blush. "Jake should really keep better track of you." He took a sip of his champagne. "Where is he, by the way? Florence said he was coming tonight."

I nodded. "He is. He had to stop by the shop, but said he'd meet me here. We haven't had a chance to talk. I told him I didn't think it was a good idea for us to come."

Stuart smiled and took my hand. "You're trembling. Don't worry, Celia, when he gets here I'll make myself scarce. Scout's honor." He raised his arm, two fingers extended in the Boy Scout salute.

I looked around. No one was paying the slightest bit of attention to us. Still, my mouth was dry and I felt lightheaded. "Is there anything to drink besides champagne?"

"There's punch. And it's not spiked—I checked." He grinned, then took my elbow and steered me to the couch. "Here, sit down. I'll get you some."

"No, I'll go with you. I'd like to get some air."

While he made his way through the crowd around the punch bowl, I slipped through the French doors and out into the cool night. Several people were leaning against the low terrace wall, laughing and smoking cigarettes. I didn't recognize them and figured that they must be colleagues of Jerry's. I moved to the far corner, next to a potted magnolia tree.

From there the city sparkled like fireflies on a summer night. The last time Jake and I were at Bear Lake he had caught some fireflies and put them in a jar. They flitted back and forth against the glass, then landed on the bottom. The translucent light disappeared. "They can only shine when they fly," Jake had said, then released them back into the night.

"A penny for your thoughts." Stuart handed me a small cut-glass cup and set another on the wall beside me. "I brought you two," he said, without waiting for an answer. "These things are so small, they can't begin to quench your thirst."

I smiled and drained the first cup. The murmur of other conversation had stopped, and I heard the French doors click as the smokers went back inside.

"Celia?" Stuart took the empty cup and set it on the wall. He stood, hands at his sides—not touching me, but just a step away. My heart leaped in response to the look in his eyes. One step: that was all that separated me from his embrace. The last time Stuart kissed me, I had run away. This time I knew I couldn't run.

"I love you, Celia." His voice was husky with desire and not a little pain.

I took the step.

The rough stucco on the terrace wall scratched my skin. I pressed against it harder, welcoming the pain. My knees were shaking, and they almost buckled as I forced myself to speak.

"I can't."

Stuart nodded, his eyes brimming with tears. "I know." He reached out and brushed my cheek with a fingertip. "If you change your mind, you know where to find me."

I closed my eyes. When I opened them again, he was gone.

I heard a car engine turn over and tires squeal on the black-top road. Noise from the house grew louder as the terrace doors opened once again.

"Celia? I got here as soon as I could." Jake stood in the doorway. He looked handsome in his three-piece suit, but tired, and somehow so afraid.

Chapter Forty-one

I cleared my throat. "I think I'd like to go home now, please."

He smiled and reached for my hand just as Florence appeared behind him. "Have either of you seen Stuart?" she asked. "Dean Braswell's been looking all over for him."

"Stuart's gone," I said without taking my eyes off my husband's face. "And I don't think he'll be back."

E p i l o g u e

I guess I thought little Jesse wouldn't notice that we never made it to Aunt Rose's grave that day. He kept quiet on the way home, but Libby phoned that night to tell me he was upset.

"He wouldn't go to bed, Mom. He finally told me he was afraid Nana Rose's feelings were hurt because she didn't get flowers like the rest."

"I'm sorry, Libby. Will it help if I talk to him?"

"No, you don't have to. I promised I'd take him back out there tomorrow. I said we'd order flowers from a shop, but he insists on picking them himself." She paused. "He wants to take roses from your garden, and I thought, since it's on the way . . ."

I smiled. "Of course. Come by anytime. Your father and I are going up to the lake for a few days, but you know where the clippers are."

For a moment I felt guilty for not going with her, but I knew for certain Aunt Rose wouldn't mind.

"Don't grieve for me," she had said on the day we found out she was going to die. "This old cancer may destroy my body, but it can't touch my soul. I'm going on to a brand-new life with Jesus in my heavenly home. Save your tears for the ones who have to stay behind."

I said goodby to Libby, hung up the phone and went on with my letter to Dotty.

Jake and I are going up to the lake tomorrow. The cabin we just bought is small, but Jake has plans to expand it. He has plans for a rose garden too. And a fishing boat, and a place to tinker with that old motorbike.

I wish you could see it. I love to walk up there—especially in the morning, when the woods are cool and the dew still makes the spider webs shine. I step through the gate onto slipper-soft moss, then pick up a path that winds past blackberry tangles and into a circle of fir and cedar and giant pines. Someday we're going to build a gazebo there.

When Jake is with me, we climb Cedar Hill. There's an ancient apple tree at the very top. It never bears, of course, but the leaves give plenty of shade on a summer afternoon. It's a good time to just be together. A time to speak of love and trust, of holding on and letting go.

Sometimes I think I could stay there forever, lying on the cool, damp grass and watching the wind shape the clouds. Jake and I still like to make up stories. About the clouds, I mean. And once in a while one of us will touch the other's hand and say, "Do you remember . . . ?"